A. E. Hotchner

KISSING THE WIND

A. E. Hotchner is the author of the international bestsellers *Papa Hemingway*, *Doris Day: Her Own Story*, *Sophia: Living and Loving*, and his own memoir, *King of the Hill*. He adapted many of Hemingway's works for the screen, and he was the founder, with Paul Newman, of Newman's Own. He died in 2020 at age 102.

D0167645

Also by A. E. Hotchner

FICTION

*The Amazing Adventures
of Aaron Broom*

Louisiana Purchase

The Man Who Lived at the Ritz

Treasure

The Dangerous American

NONFICTION

Hemingway in Love

*O.J. in the Morning,
G&T at Night*

Paul and Me

*The Good Life According
to Hemingway*

Everyone Comes to Elaine's

*Shameless Exploitation
in Pursuit of the Common Good*
(with Paul Newman)

*The Day I Fired Alan Ladd and
Other World War II Adventures*

Blown Away

Hemingway and His World

Choice People

Sophia: Living and Loving

Doris Day: Her Own Story

Looking for Miracles

King of the Hill

Papa Hemingway

KISSING THE WIND

KISSING
THE WIND

A. E. Hotchner

Anchor Books
A Division of Penguin Random House LLC
New York

AN ANCHOR BOOKS ORIGINAL, SEPTEMBER 2021

Library of Congress Cataloging-in-Publication Data
Names: Hotchner, A. E., author.
Title: Kissing the wind / A. E. Hotchner.
Description: New York : Anchor Books, a division of Penguin
    Random House LLC, 2021.
Identifiers: LCCN 2021010261 (print) | LCCN 2021010262 (ebook) |
    ISBN 9780593313763 (trade paperback) | ISBN 9780593313770 (ebook)
Classification: LCC PS3558.O8 K57 2021 (print) | LCC PS3558.O8 (ebook) |
    DDC 813/.54—dc23
LC record available at https://lccn.loc.gov/2021010261
LC ebook record available at https://lccn.loc.gov/2021010262

Anchor Books Trade Paperback ISBN: 978-0-593-31376-3
eBook ISBN: 978-0-593-31377-0

Book design by Nicholas Alguire

www.anchorbooks.com

Printed in the United States of America
10   9   8   7   6   5   4   3   2   1

To my dearest daughters, Tracie and Holly; my beloved son, Timothy; and for the love of my life, my wife, Virginia

Love seeketh not itself to please,
Nor for itself hath any care,
But for another gives its ease,
And builds a Heaven in Hell's despair.

—William Blake

INTRODUCTION

A. E. Hotchner and I met fifty-six years ago when Bennett Cerf, the founder of Random House, asked me to meet Mr. Hotchner and read his manuscript. That manuscript became *Papa Hemingway*. It was a bestseller in the United States and was published throughout the world. He went on to write nineteen more books. What follows is his last book, which he said he wrote to show couples how they could help each other, no matter what illness they had.

He had Charles Bonnet syndrome, which is explained in this book, and he died at the age of 102 in his beloved house in Westport with his wife, Virginia, and his loved ones at his side.

He was a bon vivant and a good friend and also a wicked tennis player. He will be sorely missed.

—Nan A. Talese

Part One

CHAPTER ONE

It came upon me imperceptibly, teasing me with its implications, giving me masked notice of its pervasive intentions. I had no way of perceiving that the life that I lived, nicely fashioned to my liking, was at risk.

I was a successful attorney in specialized practice. I occasionally wrote legal thrillers in my spare time, and I was blessed with a rewarding group of friends. All of it, now, in serious jeopardy because I had been unexpectedly invaded by a baffling, mystifying force that defied expulsion. That invasion was sudden, and I was not forewarned. It was so subtle I am hard put to identify when I first became aware of its presence. I'd say it was about a year ago, on a sparkling sunny morning.

I was on my way in an Uber to Charlie Epps's office in the Carriggon Building, where he was a member of the prestigious law firm of Whittiker & Sheen, which filled three floors of the building. Charlie's family and mine had occupied the same apartment complex all our lives, and our mothers were fast friends who'd shared our early days. Charlie and I went to the same schools: Robin's Nest preschool, Oak Street Elementary, Chester Arthur high school, Haverford College, and Columbia Law. But when we graduated sixteen years ago and were offered positions with Whittiker & Sheen, Charlie chose the security of the big law firm and prosperous clients. I chose to wallow in student debt, representing authors, artists, and other creatives who often paid me in galleys, tickets, and screeners. But it worked out: Whittiker & Sheen was a white-shoe corporate transactional law firm, but on the rare occasion their clients were sued they preferred not to farm out the work to another firm. I had plenty of trials under my belt, so Charlie would bring me in as "of counsel." It was a flexible affiliation that allowed my friend to toss me the occasional high-paying client to subsidize my solo First Amendment–focused practice.

I was headed on that bright spring morning to confer with Charlie on an unusual case that was right up my alley. Penelope Tee, a brilliant Singaporean novelist who specialized in magical realism, had been involved in a high-profile romance and bitter breakup that had spilled into the tabloids. Tee had maintained total silence about her private life but later published a book about an acclaimed poet who cheats on his lover with an anthropomorphized garden hedge. Many saw parallels between the main character and her ex-husband Danny Norgaard, an acclaimed poet who had been photographed getting cozy with the avant-garde horticulturalist Victoria Celluci at the Los Angeles hotspot Chi Spacca prior to the breakup. Complicating matters, the homewrecker character, Valeria Cespuglio, reads a poem in chapter 4 that is identical to Norgaard's acclaimed poem "Cacio e Pepe" save for a few scatological puns. Norgaard filed an action for libel and copyright infringement, citing damages in excess of thirty million dollars.

Tee's previous work had been well received critically, if not commercially. This book, *Topiary*, had had trouble attracting a major publisher. She wound up at Dodecahedron, a small publisher/vanity project owned by Rowena Flakfizer, CEO of Osgood Industries. Osgood was a purveyor of useful doodads, knickknacks, widgets, and what-have-yous, and Charlie's biggest client. The firm was happy to offer my reduced "of counsel" rate to defend Tee.

There was an open elevator in the busy lobby that I commandeered, and I pushed the button for Charlie's high floor. As we started upward, I became aware of an unusual sight—in the right rear corner of the elevator was a large, glossy rubber plant. Peculiar, I thought, a big rubber plant taking up the usually crowded space of an elevator. I mentioned it to Charlie when we settled down to work.

"You sure? I don't remember any rubber plants in the elevator but I'll check it out," he said.

When we left his office for lunch, Charlie preceded me into the elevator.

"Well, no rubber plant in this one, is there?"

He was right. The rubber plant was not there.

"Rubber plants are for the lobbies of cheap motels," he said.

"Well," I said, "I guess they took it out."

I let it go at that. I didn't realize it at the time, but that was the first sign of it, the scourge that would invade my life.

That evening, to my monthly regret, was an obligation to have a formal dinner and several hands of bridge at the twelve-room apartment of Lance R. A. Dixon, whom I had met when Charlie had brought me in to defend his company in a rather heated trademark dispute. Dixon was a supercharged tycoon who had decided that I was a possible mate for his daughter Violet, who was recovering from a tempestuous divorce. She was a handsome, engaging woman in her thirties, but despite Dixon's forceful machinations I was disinclined to cooperate. I had recently retreated from a rather lengthy relationship and was not eager to involve myself in tuxedo-clad bridge (which I played miserably) and country clubs. Of course Dixon was a whiz at bridge as well as golf, tennis, and playing the piano. He insisted I join his country club foursome despite my obvious shortcomings, saying, "I'll get the pro to get you up to par after the wedding."

I had tried to evade all talk of marriage, but Dixon's mind was made up. His eagerness on my behalf induced one awful result. He had maneuvered me into a doubles game at his club in the Hamptons, paired me up with one of the pros to compensate for the superior skill of him and his partner. I was playing at the net when he rose up to his full height to hit an overhead and smashed the ball right at me, smack into my right eye. I had a black eye for a week or so, but many visits to my ophthalmologist had a terrible final pronouncement: the force of Dixon's smash had irrevocably shattered my optic nerve and I would be forever blind in that eye.

Dixon's comment when I told him was, "Too bad, but listen, you have to take care of yourself. It's much worse playing football. I played every football game at Dartmouth, left tackle, and had not so much as a scratch. You learned a good tennis lesson. You see me go up for an overhead, turn your head away and cover it with your racket. I'll be your partner next time. I'm really better at doubles than the pro and I'll give you pointers during the game."

Somehow, even after all this, Dixon had still bullied me into committing myself to a dinner-and-bridge night with his wife and Violet at their apartment on the first Tuesday of every month. I had consented to please Violet, even though I am worse at bridge than at tennis. To make the evening even more objectionable, Violet let me know that her father always dined in black tie and asked me to please do likewise.

So in a grim mood, I presented my tuxedoed self for the impending bridge ordeal, but it was the dinner that got to me first. My salad was thickly covered with what looked like little clusters of pine needles. I glanced over at Violet and saw her eating her salad, which had none of these little sprigs of needles.

"Did you have the pine needles?" I whispered.

"What pine needles?"

"Like mine."

She looked at my salad.

"What pine needles? That's just arugula and slices of lobster."

I looked at my salad and saw that underneath the clusters were the arugula and lobster. I tried pushing the clusters away to get at the underneath, but the clusters wouldn't move.

"Something the matter, dear?" her mother asked Violet.

"No, Mom. It's a lovely salad."

The dinner of lamb chops, diced potatoes, and spinach had no abnormalities. But I brooded about my salad all through my bridge playing, which drew even more fire from Dixon than usual. On my way home, I was still thinking about why I couldn't move those little pine clumps with my fork. I couldn't lift them or push them aside.

When I arrived at my apartment, a lofty two-bedroom

with a study and a balcony on the thirty-seventh floor, I found more to brood about.

To begin with, there were black dots on the hall carpet outside my door and on the carpet in the bedroom and bathroom. The dots were all the same small size and certainly had not been there when I was last in the apartment. But even more disconcerting was my toilet. When I lifted the lid, the surface of the water was covered with a grid that looked metallic. I flushed the toilet but the grid remained in place.

I went to the wall phone in the living room and requested that the concierge send the handyman on duty. Salvatore showed up a few minutes later carrying a wire cutter. Sal was my favorite handyman. He was a philosopher who could recite several of Shakespeare's sonnets—in Italian, of course.

I led him to the toilet and showed him the grid. He gave a look and said, "What grid?"

"*That* grid—the one that covers the water."

There was an uncomfortable silence while he took his eyeglasses from his pocket and kneeled down to give the toilet bowl a closer inspection. As before, the grid did not move. Salvatore stood up, took off his glasses, and put them back in his pocket. He seemed embarrassed.

"Can you remove it?"

"You can use it the way it is. Perfectly okay."

The sprigs of pine needles began to creep up on me, along with a gnawing sense in my stomach that something eerie and incomprehensible was overwhelming me. Instinctively, I knew that I shouldn't pursue the subject of the grid with Salvatore.

"Thanks, Sal. So it's okay as is?"

"Yes, sir."

He was gathering up his stuff, obviously anxious to leave.

"Oh, Sal, these black dots, is this ink, maybe, or paint?"

Sal looked where I was pointing. "I wouldn't know," he said, moving to the door.

I held up the usual tip but he was already in the hall and headed toward the service elevator.

I called out to him, "Sal, you didn't see any dots or a grid, did you?"

The elevator doors slid open. "No, sir," he said as he disappeared inside.

I went back into the apartment, intent on testing the toilet. The grid was still in place. I urinated and flushed. The liquid disappeared from the bowl but the grid screen persisted. I reached my hand into the fresh toilet water and tried to grab the grid and pull it away. There was nothing to grab. The grid was on the water but there was no actual grid.

I recoiled in shock. Something ominous was obviously happening to me, but what? I was seeing things others did not see. I went into the living room and turned on the television, hoping its reality would dispel my feeling of panic. A news program flooded the room. The familiar newscasters somewhat assuaged my dread. But after a few minutes of the newscast, a well-dressed man walked into my room and came to my chair. He stood beside me and watched the program. He was tall and wore a dark suit with a yellow tie, a simple black design on it. He was an absolute stranger whom I had never seen before.

I jumped up from my chair, fear sweat breaking out on my face.

"Who the hell . . . !" I could barely gather my voice, although I tried desperately to yell. "Get out of here!"

He did not look at me, nor did his expression change. He wore an expensive wristwatch and a gold ring on one of his little fingers.

I went to my apartment's wall telephone. "I'm calling for help!" I grabbed the phone from the wall. Not looking at me, the man turned around and left, but I did not hear the front door open or close. I searched around to be sure, but he had left, all right. There was no sign of anything missing nor of his having been there.

CHAPTER TWO

Next morning, first thing, I made an appointment with our family doctor, Louis Litman, an extraordinary man who had watched over my well-being all my life. He had been a devoted friend of my father's and was a man of years—eighty-eight, I'd guess—who dispatched healthy wisdom as well as prescriptions. The tragic loss of my father, a father who had been a close and vital part of my life, had prompted Doc Lou to keep an eye on me.

"Well, Chet," Doc Lou said with his gravelly voice, "it's about time something's gone kerplunk with you."

I was in no mood for our usual banter but went right into the onslaught of events that had bedeviled me, from the rubber plant in the elevator with its connected tendrils to the pine clusters in the salad, the grating over the water in my toilet, the black dots all over the carpets, the stranger in my apartment.

"Unnerving things, and I'm spooked, Doc Lou."

"Well, you may have had a tiny stroke. That may account for it. Let's take a look at you."

He gave me a thorough examination, stethoscoping my back with deep breaths, checking my heart, lungs, hearing, eyes, oxygen level, and blood pressure, and taking blood samples, the whole medical works.

"Not a ripple, Chet. But maybe the lab'll turn up something. Meanwhile, I think you should get an MRI of your brain and have the brain boys take a look. You ever had an MRI?"

"Nope."

"It's a little spooky. They seal you into this coffin like a mummy and churn eerie noises at you." He picked up his phone and made an MRI appointment for me. "I'll be in touch when I get the results."

"Thanks, Doc Lou."

He scribbled on his prescription pad and tore one off for me. "All right, take one of these anti-worries at bedtime. You remember the time you came to me with your pal Charlie, when you two were the basketball backcourt for Haverford and you had an ankle the size of an aggravated salami and you were worried you'd have to miss the championship game?"

I had to laugh. "And you gave me an anti-worry lollipop and a shot in my ankle before the game."

"And you guys were phenomenal! I felt pride in your ankle every time you scored a basket. So my advice is, go do the MRI and tonight take a good shot of bourbon and one of my pills, and let me do the worrying."

CHAPTER THREE

As Doc Lou had predicted, I felt like a mummy when I was strapped into the MRI's cylindrical casket by two white-garbed men who told me not to move after the lid was closed, entombing me. The padded top was only an inch or two above my face. A deep throbbing sound flooded the space, accompanied by a voice that said to stay motionless. A high-pitched whining sound joined in, and the MRI took off! I had expected a stationary experience but to my rather frightened amazement the MRI bolted forward toward a canal of water that appeared before me. It charged right up to the edge, threatening me with immersion, then spinning away at the last second, running alongside the canal, weaving around obstacles while I shriveled in fright, unable to process what was happening, on the verge of passing out, feeling a kind of suffocation, until we suddenly stopped, the throbbing sounds turned off, and the cover of the MRI raised as the white-garbed men pushed a pedestal up to the hatch for me to use for departure. I inspected the MRI, which was now as solidly affixed to its base on the floor as it had been before, and there was no evidence of its having been anywhere. I wanted to ask the attendants about my wild ride but they were already busy prepping for the next patient.

I had tickets for the theater that evening, but I decided I had had enough drama for the day and gifted them to Charlie. When I saw him I gave a moment's thought to confiding in him, but I found myself in a kind of embarrassment about describing the events that were troubling me and said nothing. So we had a quick drink and he left to collect his wife while I stayed on, ordered a fresh gin and tonic, and faced the prospect of an evening spent alone, brooding about my whirling MRI adventure. I considered calling Doc Lou on his cell phone but instead ordered another gin and tonic and attacked the bar bowl of peanuts.

While diminishing the peanuts, I found myself dwelling angrily on my Dixon entrapment. I came to the conclusion that I had to put a definite end to my uncommitted engagement to Violet and to all involvement with Dixon's tennis and bridge and everything else Dixonian.

Doc Lou called the following day to report on my MRI. "So, Chet, your brain is A-okay, no sign of any lesions from mini-strokes or anything else."

I was a bit disappointed, hoping there would be some evidence to explain the freaky nature of my recent encounters.

I told him about my wild ride in the MRI machine.

"It took you all over the place and skidded around watery canals?" There was a long pause on the telephone. "I think the best thing now, Chet, is for you to see a good neurologist who is better equipped than I am to deal with your special problems. I know one of the best, Dr. Alexander Brevoro. He is in demand, long wait list, but I can get you an appointment. What do you say?"

"Please do. The sooner, the better."

I hunkered down in my apartment that evening, boldly turning on the lights and hanging up my jacket. The music channel was playing on television, Mozart. I went to turn it off, only to discover it had not been turned on. And yet channel 899 was playing. This was not a day for my cleaning woman, besides which Glenda had never ever turned on the television. She also despised what she called "long-haired pussy music." I turned the set on and off and Mozart departed.

Two flowering bushes had been planted in the living room carpet, but I didn't make any effort to get rid of them.

I made myself a drink and turned on an evening news program. As the anchor came on, so did a troupe of children who bunched themselves beside the television screen to watch the picture. They were very well-dressed boys and girls who made no sounds, none at all. The children were a little strange but not identifiable. I tried to shoo them away, waving my hands at them and shouting, but they didn't look in my direction. I took a candle from its holder and tried to poke it at them, but they skillfully avoided it as they moved away from the living room. I got up to see where they were going but they simply disappeared through the front door even though it was closed and locked.

I stifled a strong urge to go out to dinner and calm my galloping nerves ("You never fix a problem by running away from it") and resignedly took a bag from the fridge that contained my take-out dinner from Citarella.

I was awarded an evening devoid of interruption, but when I went to the bathroom before going to bed, the grid had returned to the toilet bowl and a cover of white feathers had obstructed the mirror over the sink. I tried to wipe them off but no amount of rubbing could remove them.

I went to bed early, not turning off the end tables' lamps and donning a pair of sleep masks, one on top of the other.

Despite my precautions, a few minutes after I had slipped under the covers, an unending file of children began to pass by me. They did not look directly at me but held hands and moved in a rhythmic way. They seemed to communicate but made no conversational sounds or laughter or singing.

I watched them as they left my bedroom and headed to the windows of the living room, where they seemed to disappear through the cracks between the molding and the glass. Looking at them, I felt a kind of paralysis. These were not figments: they were fully dimensioned children. I felt a rising panic in my body that shortened my breath and dried my mouth. There was no one I could call. There was no one who would believe me. No one who would see what I was seeing. With great effort, I forced myself to turn off the lights and take out the vial of sleeping pills that Doc Lou had given me. I swallowed the pills but my mind was of a blackness that the thought of swallowing all the rest of them crossed my mind.

I lay there in the dark, my panicky mind fighting the pills. I took two more and only then induced myself to fall asleep, thereby escaping for the time being from my dread and confusion.

CHAPTER FOUR

Dr. Alexander Brevoro was younger than I had expected, a handsome man in his late forties, I'd say, with a close-cropped beard and remarkable, penetrating deep-set eyes. His office was simply furnished, with no framed diplomas on the walls. Just seascapes and moonlit clouds.

Dr. Brevoro asked me a few questions about my combined life as attorney and mystery writer but seemed more interested in the writing part of it. In a painful piece of irony, my recurring character was a blind Black man named Jefferson Honeywell, who solved difficult cases with the help of his remarkable Bedlington terrier. Honeywell was fashioned after an extraordinary blind student who was in my law class and ranked in the high fives. Yet ever since the tennis incident, when I had half-joined Honeywell and his inspiration, my creative drive had dried up.

Perhaps sensing my pain around the subject, Dr. Brevoro transitioned to asking me to describe the incidents that Doc Lou had mentioned to him. He said he had scheduled me as the day's last appointment so I'd have plenty of time.

I started with the strange appearance in my apartment, then the grid on my toilet and the children parading by my bed but not looking at me. I was in the middle of my recounting the MRI voyage when he interrupted:

"Tell me about your eyes."

"My eyes?"

"Yes. How are your eyes?"

"Well . . . I have them but the right one doesn't function."

"You're totally blind in that eye?"

"Yes."

"Since when? Birth?"

"No. Recently. I got blasted in my right eye with an overhead tennis shot. Why do you ask?"

"My initial impression, which I will have to corroborate, is that you have Charles Bonnet syndrome."

"What is that?"

"A very rare affliction that primarily occurs in older people who are blind or partially blind. Not much is known about it even among doctors. Dr. Litman, for example, never heard of it. It happens to be something that as a neurologist interests me. I have had Charles Bonnet patients who are visited at night by crowds of children, by intruders with bizarre, distorted faces, by beautifully gowned women who dance exotically by waving silk scarves that turn into rabbits. All of them were blind or partially blind, and elderly. And I have had patients who are middle-aged and suffer macular degeneration. But none as young as you, and it remains to be seen what your Charles Bonnet is going to inflict on you. For it is, no doubt, a form of torture that you can only treat by fighting your hallucinations with a strong instinctual awareness, convincing yourself that what is happening to you is stemming from a brain that is rebelling against its deprivation of sight in that eye."

"Are you telling me," I said, "that all I can do to fight off this onslaught is to try to convince myself that it is not real?"

"I'm afraid it is. There is no known cure, no medicine that reaches it. Various remedies have been tried, but none have had any effect whatsoever. There have been attempts to fiddle with the brain and they have made the Bonnet even worse for those who have tried it."

"Who was this Charles Bonnet?"

"He was a Swiss naturalist who lived in the eighteenth century and specialized in early research in photogenesis, psychology, and eventually philosophy. But his interest in hallucinations began when his grandfather Charles Lullin started to experience 'visions' when his eyesight began to fail. Bonnet asked him to keep a day-to-day account of his hallucinations. This was around 1750. Over the ensuing years, Lullin took his task very seriously and filled pages and pages with accounts of his hallucinations. Bonnet came to the conclusion that it was the brain that was the source of those hallucinations, and when Bonnet himself developed partial blindness and suffered hallucinations similar to his grandfather's, he was able to identify those visions as uniquely more dimensional and more serious than others. Unfortunately, Lullin's valuable account was lost for one hundred and fifty years. It wasn't until the 1990s that Bonnet syndrome really started finding its way into medical books, and Lullin's hallucinations became medical history."

I was dumbfounded by this unexpected reality. A future filled with children at my television, parading around my bedroom, joining me at a restaurant. Strangers participating in every aspect of my life. The bathroom, the kitchen, my home in Connecticut—everywhere I went, they too would go. And this might be just the beginning. Ahead of me might be a future with awful assaults, even worse than what I had already experienced.

"I'm afraid all I can do is to help you keep protecting yourself with the reality that your brain is creating the hallucinations, that they're not something generated by mysterious outside forces with a reality of their own. That is the essence of Charles Bonnet syndrome."

"Then by coming here . . ."

"I will analyze your experiences with you to keep you holding on to the reality of who you are and what you are. Otherwise, on your own, the Bonnet syndrome is so realistic it can cause a destructive negativism. There have been suicides . . ."

"You paint a terrible future for me."

"I hope not. Your future is susceptible to your power over yourself to adapt. Also, it often happens that the Bonnet rescinds or abates for a while, sometimes for years."

"But it can return?"

"Maybe. Maybe not. Depends on how lucky you are."

He accompanied me to the door. We shook hands. He did not look positive. I did not feel lucky.

CHAPTER FIVE

I left Dr. Brevoro's office feeling that an essential part of me had been removed, or rather had withered and died. A life infected with Bonnet syndrome, impervious to any known treatments, what little hope there was confined to the intervention of luck.

I couldn't focus on where to go to try to straighten out my mind. I moved along with the flow of the passing crowd, stopping at the corner. When the sign turned to "Walk" I didn't cross the street with the waiting group but stayed rooted while several "Walk" signs changed. I was desperately trying to get hold of myself. Finally, I became aware of where I was and realized I was only a few blocks from Central Park. I headed to the Ramble, an unkempt woodland section I often visited, and found a secluded bench beside a mound of logs. Squirrels were busy and a couple of pigeons came up to me seeking handouts.

Well, Chet, I thought, *you might as well face the facts: it all stems from Dixon deliberately and fatally blasting your right eye.* That was all the invitation Bonnet syndrome needed to move in and do its dirty work. And that was only the beginning: with only one eye to guide me, I'd had to give up driving my car because the insurance company wouldn't cover me; for movies and plays, I had to always get seats in the center or the right orchestra; at dinner parties I had to surreptitiously switch the name cards to put my preferred seatmate to my left. And now, with the Bonnet spooking my food, I would have to start declining all invitations.

It was time to put my house in order. Dixon and Violet had to go, right away. And the country club! And nighttime activities would have to be reduced as much as possible, since the dark nurtures the activities of Bonnet syndrome. I was alone in this. I could not call for help. There was no help. I had to meet it head-on.

I felt the semblance of a tear in my good eye as a ball came bouncing up to me with a little boy chasing after it. He was wearing a Yankees shirt and cap and a baseball glove on his left hand. I flipped the ball to him and he caught it with his glove.

"Sorry to bother you, sir," he said.

"What's your name?"

"Jack."

"Good name."

"If it's my mom. John, if it's my father."

"They don't agree?"

"Nope. You wanna play catch?"

I stood up and he threw me the ball, a rubberized version of a baseball, and I pitched it back to him.

"Hey, you're a good thrower." He zipped it back to me. "You play? Are you a baseball player?" We began to toss the ball back and forth.

"In college I pitched and my best buddy was my catcher."

"You hit any home runs?"

"Not many. My buddy hit the homers."

"Can you curve and do sliders and knuckleballs?"

"Are you a pitcher?"

"No, sir. It's shortstop for me. I'm very fast." He took off full speed and circled back, throwing the ball to me as he slid to the bench. A young woman with short blond hair, carrying a few of what I surmised were Jack's belongings, appeared.

"Has he pestered you into becoming a Yankee?" she asked, trailing laughter.

"John-Jack is about ready for the big leagues, isn't he?" I said.

"He knows how to curve and throw sliders and knuckleballs," John-Jack said admiringly.

"I can see he's turned his baseballese on you," the young woman said.

"He's my friend," the boy declared. "We're having a great catch."

"No you're not," his mother said. "We're late. I couldn't find you."

"Oh, Mom . . ."

"Another time, John-Jack," I said. "I come here often. Okay? But don't try throwing a curve, your arm's not ready for it."

"Mom, how about five minutes more?"

"No minutes more. Thank the nice man for playing catch."

"Oh, all right. I'll look for you when I come . . ."

I threw him the ball and he nestled it in the pocket of his glove. His mom smiled at me, a wonderful smile, and they left, John-Jack's mother with her arm around his Yankee shoulders.

I watched them going over the Bow Bridge and over Cherry

Hill and in the direction of the looming beauty of Belvedere Castle. I sat down hard on the bench. A little boy like that, and a wife like that . . . I always thought those things would eventually be mine, but not now. Not under the curse of Bonnet syndrome.

"No!" I exploded as I popped up from the bench, frightening an elderly couple passing by. "No!" I recalled Dr. Brevoro telling me this was all just my brain rebelling against my injured eye. I repeated it aloud. "It's just my brain!" I threw my coat over my shoulder, loosened my collar, and headed for the West Side exit by way of Turtle Pond.

CHAPTER SIX

It was Violet's thirty-sixth birthday and Daddy Dixon was giving her a posh party at Table 49, a highly touted Chinese restaurant in Columbus Circle that featured ostentatious Asian fusion cuisine and extravagant tabs. The décor was starkly modern interrupted with touches of Ming dynasty objets. Not really the proper setting for announcing my impending departure, but it had to be done. I had to totally simplify my life if I was going to be able to accommodate the bizarre Bonnet people and events that were to fill it from now on.

I did regret having to be so abrupt and final with Violet. She really was a very thoughtful and beautiful woman, witty and outgoing, but the fact was we had never struck any sparks and I should have admitted it long ago. Besides, how would I ever accommodate her obeisance to her father—or my own?

The birthday table was in a desirable alcove of the restaurant facing the likeness of Christopher Columbus in the circle below. I was seated next to Violet, Papa Dixon on the other side of her. There were ten people at the table: the Dixons, a couple of relatives, Violet's friends, and me. Wine was being poured, but I noticed there were several of those damn pine sprigs in my glass. I knew the sprigs couldn't be seen by anyone but me, but I passed on the wine and ordered a double vodka martini to fuel my resolve. Exotic hors d'oeuvres were being passed and the table was coming to life. Birthday toasts were being offered and Violet was responding happily. My resolve to make this night my getaway began to weaken: *Maybe not on her birthday, maybe I should wait until tomorrow.* I took a liberal pull of my martini and, to my amazement, saw a long file of people coming into our alcove. There were beautifully costumed dancers, four women who waved their lavender scarves like birds above their heads, young people in festive dress who crowded around me, and some men whose clothes looked European. None of them were talking or singing or making any noise whatsoever. I tried to wave away some of those pushing in on me but I couldn't make contact, and when I tried to look them in the face they turned their heads away. I mumbled something at them, at the same time trying to hear Dr. Brevoro's *It's just your brain*, but it did no good. The oppression around this room full of arriving celebrants was so real it overwhelmed me, and even though Violet was alarmed by my behavior, I couldn't control myself.

I realized Violet was pulling at my sleeve to stop me from waving my shooing hand at the interlopers, whom, of course, she couldn't see.

"What's happening, what's wrong?" she kept saying.

A group of six identical dancers waving fans was moving around me.

Dixon got up and came over. The whole table was now aware of my antics. Dixon leaned over me. "What in the devil's going on?" he said.

"All right, listen," I said, knowing that my time had come,

"please sit down, Mr. Dixon. I have something to explain about myself. I'm sorry it comes on your birthday, Violet."

Two waiters entered pushing carts that contained an assortment of the restaurant's signature dishes.

A quiet hum had descended over the table. Dixon returned to his seat without commenting. The waiters distributed their dishes.

"Okay, Chet," Dixon said as soon as they departed. "Let's hear your sob story."

I gave him a hard look. "Well, it begins with you, Mr. Dixon," I said, "that time you socked me with a tennis ball and it left me blind in my right eye."

Dixon pounded his fist on the table, making the plates jump. "It was an ordinary overhead you should have avoided!"

I pressed on. "I healed up and that should have been the end of it, just learning to get along with one eye, but I was terribly unlucky—only a limited number of people who are blind or half-blind contract what is known as Charles Bonnet syndrome, and I am one of these unlucky ones. The syndrome produces hallucinations that are more realistic than any other hallucinations, having fully dimensional people, animals, places—a whole world that only the affected person can see. Right now, in this room, all around us, are festive people in bright seductive clothing, closing in on me. I am trying to disperse them but they are not susceptible to touch or speech. They make no sound, they don't speak or sing, but they can create and drive cars and trains. Strange birds will fly and weird animals will prowl; there might be women floating in the air and fish that can function on land, all kinds of animals à la Marc Chagall—a whole world created by your brain that you are hostage to. The worst of it is that there is no known cure or remedy or even a partial alleviation for this cruel affliction. Wherever you are, wherever you go, this syndrome can submerge you in its self-serving world and take you away from yours. I will try to carry on my profession to whatever extent I can, but I must give up any hope for a normal life, a family, children . . . any kind of commitment is not to be. This is a painful message that I have to give you, Violet, especially on your birthday, but I cannot be anything else than honest. When I go home tonight, I'll probably be beset by strange and disturbing things the Bonnet has unleashed. That is my way of life now, and it is not a life into which I can bring anyone, especially someone I love." The lie left my lips uneasily, but the confession itself had left me in a sweat, as had the Bonnet-built bodies still pressing in all around me, so hopefully it seemed only one more strangeness among the rest. "Goodbye to everyone. I hope you understand I must ride this one out alone."

Dixon jumped to his feet. "What is all this rubbish about hallucinations of the blind?" he thundered. "I don't see any beauties prancing around with flying ribbons!"

One of the guests held up his iPhone. "It's in here, Dix," he said, and he read: " 'Charles Bonnet syndrome is a type of psychophysical visual disturbance and the experience of complex visual hallucinations in a person with partial or severe blindness.' "

"Lemme see that!" Dixon shouted, snatching the phone.

I moved away from the table and headed toward the outer stairs. I could hardly move my frozen legs. As I started down, the Bonnet intruders began to disappear. I had just experienced the most harrowing moment of my life: the look on Violet's face. I needed to collect myself. There was an Irish bar directly across the street from the restaurant. I stumbled in and settled at the bar with a double bourbon. There was anonymous music but thankfully no television. I became aware someone was slipping onto the stool next to mine. In the mirror behind the bar I saw Violet.

"I want one of those," she said, indicating my drink. I signaled the bartender. Violet and I clinked glasses.

"You've got to understand I love you and it doesn't matter to me if there are hallucinations or anything else. I will be there to take care of you."

I was surprised and touched by the depth of her devotion. In the past months, I'd felt Violet's father's passion more strongly than her own. But the honest truth of her feelings didn't alter mine—or the lack thereof. Moreover, it could do nothing to change the circumstances.

I sipped my drink and turned to look at her. "That is lovely to hear, but there is no way we could share a life. Children would not be possible. These creatures will affect every part of my existence. They are just getting started. No telling how far they will go. I don't doubt that you love me but what will be happening to me will not be happening to you. They will be carrying me off but you will not be with me. Unable to do anything to rescue me. Now, difficult as it is, I am subject to a form of life imprisonment, and you must recognize that it is life imprisonment without visiting hours."

"But can't we give it a try? Please?"

"No. All I can do is try to survive this demonic ordeal. And I must put all of me into that."

"Yes, and I will help you."

"How? As a young widow?"

I finished my drink and signaled for another.

She was crying softly.

"I was counting on you," she said.

"For what?"

"That we'd marry and I could get away from my father. He wrecked my first marriage but I thought you might have the guts to stand up to him."

It was shaming to think how little that had been the case. But it made me even surer that I had to focus on Violet's feelings now, not my own. "Listen, Violet," I told her, "listen: you are an attractive thirty-six-year-old woman and all you have to do is find a nice apartment, fix it up the way you like, and tell Daddy you'll be leaving his employ because you're going to be living and working on your own."

"Working on my own? Doing what?"

"You're a hell of a designer."

"But that was long ago . . ."

A man in a black suit and tie came into the bar.

"I'll be right out, Tommy," Violet said. She had stopped crying.

She slid off her seat and I walked her out to the Cadillac at the curb. Tommy opened the door and she curled up in a corner of the backseat. The driver got behind the wheel and I watched the Dixon license plate disappear into the night.

CHAPTER SEVEN

I had spent the better part of a year trying to resolve the Tee lawsuit. One front was a case of libel-in-fiction, whereby Norgaard would have to prove that readers would understand the book to be a thinly veiled roman à clef with the main character, Dante Bragaard, as a stand-in for Norgaard, and that furthermore, unlike his literary counterpart, he did *not* have an affair with Celluci/Cespuglio. Tee was intensely private and reluctant to tell me, even in confidence under our attorney-client privilege, anything about the affair. I had pressed her to present evidence so that it would not merely be her word against Norgaard's.

Then there was the copyright infringement claim, where I would have to make a compelling argument that the use of Norgaard's verse was justified under fair use or the First Amendment right to parody. While Tee's defacing of "Cacio e Pepe" was quite funny, if a little juvenile, it was hard to argue that replacing "*cacio e pepe*" with "*cacca e pipì*" throughout the poem was protected artistic expression.

Further complicating matters, Flakfizer and Tee were

dead set against any offer of settlement, for different reasons. Tee refused to retreat from the literal as well as artistic truth behind her work. Flakfizer just didn't want to pay any money if she could avoid it. Despite being wealthy beyond comprehension, she was a notorious tightwad—especially when it came to Dodecahedron. She wanted me to knock this case out on summary judgment, which meant I would have to convince a judge that scat parody is so artistic and transformative that no jury would disagree, as well as find some kind of evidence of an affair.

Suffice it to say, the case seemed destined for a trial with an uncertain outcome, but not before a host of interminable depositions in cramped conference rooms. First up was Norgaard, who would be accompanied by his pit bull legal team, headed by law partners Tina Shore and Tim Manning of Shore & Manning. If I could get him to admit he'd stepped out on Penelope, it would be game over for at least half the lawsuit, as truth is an absolute defense to libel.

Charlie had prepped me all week, pretending to be Norgaard so we could simulate my line of questioning. He was pretty good at it for someone whose only experience pretend-litigating was our Columbia Law School mock trial competition, which we would have won as partners if not for a tricky fact pattern involving the rule against perpetuities.

I had not yet told Charlie about my syndrome. I wasn't intending to keep it from him; I'd simply decided it would be better to tell him after, once I'd had a chance to prove I hadn't lost my fastball. We took our seats in a small conference room at the Whittiker & Sheen office. Flanking Norgaard were Shore and three junior associates, a paralegal, and a summer intern whom one of the associates excoriated for not wearing a tie, out of, she seemed to assume, my earshot. The plaintiff's team was total overkill, a show of force made comical by the fact that the conference room was practically the size of a walk-in closet. A court reporter sat at the short edge of the rectangular table after helping himself to a cucumber water and danish. I adjusted my chair next to Charlie's and gave him a quiet "don't worry, I got this" look. He gave me a thumbs-up back.

The court reporter cracked each knuckle individually and asked for everyone to introduce themselves for the record and to give him their business card.

"Chester Tremaine for the defendant, Penelope Tee."

As the others introduced themselves, the reporter's nimble fingers pranced across a small dictation keyboard and I found myself getting lost in the gentle clattering sound. Suddenly I looked across the table and the room had grown even more crowded. Now Manning was there as well, plus five junior associates and three summer interns. Or maybe it was four junior associates and four summer interns? I was pretty sure the paralegal was the same. Rattled, I looked at the court reporter.

"Excuse me . . ."

"Yes, counselor?"

"Would you please read that back to me?"

"Read what back?"

"The . . . names?"

"Uh, sure, no problem."

The reporter dutifully recited the introductions offered by opposing counsel so I could determine whether Manning was actually there. I didn't fret over the extra phantom associates because underlings don't speak during depositions anyway.

"What's going on?" Charlie asked, close to my ear. Did he psychically intuit my unease, or did my flop sweat give it away? Either way, I missed whether the reporter said Manning's name.

I patted Charlie's arm in indication that all was well. But it wasn't. It had registered with me that this was a syndrome intrusion, but I was upset by the daring of this invasion. I tried to focus, starting in with the usual questions: name, occupation, professional history. Just as I turned the page to my outline, a kaleidoscope of butterflies leapt off my binder. I couldn't make out the queries underneath. I did my best to recall my plan of attack, but it was all so overwhelming. I had to get to Norgaard's romantic history.

"Uh, would you consider yourself faithful?"

Manning theatrically leapt out of his seat to object, waving his arms frantically.

"Excuse me, a simple objection would suffice."

Norgaard asked, "Me? I haven't even answered yet."

"No, your attorney."

Norgaard turned to a confused Shore, who said, "I didn't say anything."

"Not you, uh, the other one."

I gestured toward Manning, but in his place was the paralegal.

It was clear that I was jumping at shadows.

"Can we go off the record for a moment?" Charlie interjected.

"Off the record at ten fifty-two a.m."

"I don't know about you all, but we've been at it for a while and I need a comfort break." That's lawyer code for going to the bathroom. "Can I get ten minutes?"

"No problem," Shore replied.

"We'll pick up at eleven oh two a.m.," said the court reporter.

Team Norgaard exchanged a couple confused looks, then filed out of the conference room to confer. It was like being on the inside of a clown car as the dozen faux associates and interns trailed out of the room. As soon as they were gone, Charlie pulled me into his office and asked me what had just happened.

Hesitatingly—but aware of the time limit my past passivity had put on this conversation—I told him all about the syndrome, Dr. Brevoro's bleak predictions, the divestment of the Dixons, the state of my life. When I was done, Charlie pinched his nose and took a heavy breath; I could sense his frustration—with the timing, the situation, or me, I was afraid to guess. But then he started talking and was immediately the devoted friend he had been all my life. He vowed to help me fight my way out of this terrible trap. The case seemed to be far from his first concern. "Lydia and I will make sure you have a social life," Charlie promised. "No way I let you withdraw and cut off everything and everybody. You may think you've lost the human race, but listen, to me the only way you lose is if you give up. Fetal position in a dark corner. Remember how we were twenty-two points down to Swarthmore? Two minutes to go, the championship game, the trophy staring us in the face—"

I interrupted him with a giant affectionate bear hug. "I'm not giving up, Charlie, believe me. But how do you win a fight if you don't know who you're fighting?"

Still, I told him I didn't want to give up my litigation work with him—that would be surrendering to the syndrome's spooks.

With Charlie's encouragement, I did my best to muddle through the remainder of the deposition, but I couldn't nail down any promising leads and Norgaard had been well coached to duck my jabs with a combination of circumspect answers and strategic forgetfulness. With all the distractions in the room, it was all I could do to hold it together without laughing or crying. And without the aid of my outline, which was still swarming with butterflies, my wild-stab questions were far too easy for Norgaard to parry. He eventually ran out the clock before I could make any headway. And that was the end of any prospects for a successful summary judgment motion—this thing was now trial or bust.

CHAPTER EIGHT

We were in a subdued mood when Lydia—lovely and amusing, the perfect wife for Charlie—joined us for dinner at Orso. She had recently shared the happy news of her pregnancy, so she didn't partake in the wine with us. Meanwhile, I skipped having salad, so the pine sprigs only appeared in the bread basket.

Charlie told Lydia about my changed circumstances, making it sound somewhat hopeful. I went back to my place feeling—if not encouraged, then at least less alone. But the minute I put my foot in the door, I realized I was going to be in forced company of a very different sort. The television was playing a channel I never watch, with a cadre of spectators clustered in front of it. They were wearing matching clothes with an identical yellow and black design. I turned off the television and without looking at me, they all headed toward the front door and disappeared without opening it.

As I walked across the thick living room carpet I noticed that the usual flat surface was now disrupted by multiple abrupt drops and swoops. Of course I told myself it was per-

fectly safe and stable and all else was an illusion. I told myself
I should not hesitate, but walk right back on top of all these
seeming impediments. Nevertheless, I walked on them with
hesitancy and fear.

In the bathroom, I not only had the same grid covering the
toilet bowl water, but there were tumbling capital letters embossed all over the floor, quickly changing into make-believe
words: MVAQRU7TOR, GRUW109ZPQ, and the like. One
moving group looked like it was trying to spell my name, getting to CHE before adding VR997QX and SWIRLINGINT,
then swirling into several other groups of words that do not
exist in any language.

I went into the living room and, not turning on the lights,
sat down in my favorite chair, intent on figuring out how I
could improve my response to the aggressively proceeding
situation. From what had happened so far, I had decided the
syndrome was much more active and threatening at night
than during the light of day, as if it prospered under cover
of darkness.

I turned the lights full on, and the light induced them to
leave.

It was not like a dream. There was no preamble, no percep-
tion of going to sleep. No, this was being doused in an experience with no introduction other than feeling a tightening on
my wrists and feet and sudden awareness that I was in a large
wooden crate, my hands and feet bound, heavy locks on the
door, spaces between the wood slats of the crate.

I could not move, but looking through the crate openings I
could see that I was in a huge warehouse. There was a wooden

box on the floor of the crate, facing me, and chipmunks were running out of it and over my legs on their way out of the crate. They did not stop on my body or show any interest in me but I felt fearful when the flow of chipmunks changed to hamsters, who passed higher up my body, their feet scratching my face. I cried out for help, but there was no response. The hamsters emerged from the box unendingly and I intensified my calls for aid. I tried to loosen my bindings but I couldn't get them to give at all.

A man came into view, well dressed, something about him familiar. As he moved closer I identified him as the handsome man I'd encountered watching television in my apartment. I called out to him, but he didn't even look at me, gave no sign that he was actually aware of me; in fact he wore the same blank look he had when he was in my apartment. The flow of hamsters suddenly abated and was replaced by small white mice, who ran around the crate and all over me, going in and out of their box but not scampering out of the crate. It was too much; angrily, I tried to swat down any who ventured too close to my bound wrists.

A horde of people appeared in the area beyond my crate, and as they walked past, I shouted a plea for help. They, too, did not look at me, nor even in my direction. They also didn't make a sound, although they were animated, were well dressed, and seemed to be enjoying themselves.

With their arrival, the mice scurried back into their box and stayed there. After the crowd passed by, the lights began to slowly fade and the crate became pitch-black. My hands had turned numb from being bound, and a fear rose in me that I might not survive. I tried to contradict my feeling of pending doom by dredging up Dr. Brevoro's advice, but the reality of my bound body, my aching ribs, and this intractable crate with its double locks thwarted my efforts. I closed my eyes and tried to clear my mind.

Surrendering to nothingness, I was rewarded with a band of brilliant light that swept me from the crate into my bed in my apartment. Panting, I checked down the length of my body: my hands were fine, not numb nor swollen, and none of me showed any effects from the ordeal in the crate. But I was trembling, and it took two of Doc Lou's sleeping pills to help me go to sleep.

CHAPTER NINE

In my weekly session with Dr. Brevoro, we analyzed my crate experience and he compared it to hallucinations some of his other patients had experienced.

"Yours is the most aggressive, the most imaginative of any of them. It may be the result of your own combative attitude toward the Bonnet syndrome."

"So my own brain is striking back at me?"

"Crazy as that may seem."

"Are you suggesting I should be more friendly toward the hell the syndrome is raising in my life?"

"No, you have to deal with it in any way you can to reduce its effect on you. You have my private number and I am certainly available to talk to you any time the Bonnet is overpowering you. But you've got to maintain your balance."

"Easier said than done, isn't it?"

In the wake of my crate experience I decided to trim the fat off the bones of my existence the best I could. To that end

I asked Charlie to come to my office and talk about my participation in any future trials. I constructed a couple of martinis and we sat at my desk with them and a bowl of Virginia peanuts while I recounted my crate assault, feeling that he was perhaps the only person who would understand what the Bonnet syndrome was inflicting on me.

"Did you have any idea where you were?" he asked.

"None whatsoever. That's what I want to talk to you about. Dr. Brevoro says it will probably intensify, that I should get myself prepared for its increased onslaughts. That's what he's observed in other patients, but he's never had any patient so intensely assaulted as me."

"I thought you were going to stand up to them and try to fight them off."

"The crate has changed my mind. It's like being on the back of a bucking steer. Just try to hold on for ten seconds before he bucks you off. Best I can do, I now figure, is limit the areas the syndrome can get at me. And cross-examination, as we've already seen, is a task it can exploit. It could cause enough trouble for me to jeopardize my legal status."

"But even your own practice occasionally takes you into litigation."

"Yes, but few of them make it to trial. They either settle or I get it tossed with a motion to dismiss."

"I don't want to lose you, Chet. Not your talent or our experience of working together."

"Nor do I. But under this duress I am no longer a reliable partner. We blew our shot at getting the case tossed at the summary judgment stage. I hope we keep up our lunches."

"Of course," said Charlie reassuringly. He looked like he wanted to say more but couldn't land on what.

"And if you need someone to take my place for the trial," I continued briskly, "how about Mary Oakes? She beat us in the mock trial competition and she has her own thriving practice."

"She'd be fine, but isn't she quite busy with her Me Too clients?"

"Not that busy. I see her once in a while. Why don't I give her a call and invite her to our usual place for a drink?"

I asked my assistant Terry to get Mary on the line for me.

"I'll try her now."

I found Mary at the Oak Room of the Plaza Hotel on Fifth Avenue. She was a tall woman with a hearty laugh and a sharp tongue. I asked her if she'd consider coming on as trial chair for the Tee case.

"I know it's probably a dud, but if you can snatch victory from the jaws of defeat I'm sure the firm would be grateful and send more work your way."

Mary smiled with her mouth but not her eyes. Before she could say no, I blurted, "Think it over, no pressure," and made a hasty retreat.

I left the Oak Room bar and started to cross the avenue, but halfway across the street the numbers on the walk sign suddenly ran out and it turned to a red "Stop," releasing the throbbing mass of waiting cars right toward me.

I was hypnotized by the charge of approaching headlights and I froze, expecting the worst. Instead, the cars slowed down and moved around me. The passing drivers did not excoriate me angrily, shaking their fists, but rather accepted my presence as part of everyday travel, elegantly skating around me like Olympic ice dancers performing a practiced routine, all while I stood there, still as a statue, in the middle of Fifth Avenue.

I was at my desk with Charlie, having our drinks, munching peanuts.

"Mary Oakes isn't available, Chet," Terry said. "Her assistant says she's in Chicago." I wobbled for a moment, trying to focus. "Shall I leave word?" Terry was asking.

I struggled to catch my breath. "Yes, ask her to call Charlie Epps when she gets back."

"Thanks, Chet," Charlie said. "What's with you? You look shook."

"I just spoke to Mary at the Oak Room bar. She's thinking it over." I finished my drink, made us two more.

"Oh, my God," Charlie said. "More syndrome hocus-pocus?"

"I never left here, did I?"

"No."

"Or get caught in oncoming traffic?"

"No. Is the syndrome interfering with your work?"

"No, so far I've been solid—except at the Norgaard deposition, of course. But now . . . I hope I can keep it secure."

"Lydia and I will see you in the country as often as usual I hope."

He was referring to the fact that we both had places in a little Connecticut town about an hour from New York, his an attractive place on the water, mine a small gardener's cottage.

"Are you coming out this weekend?" I could tell he wanted me to say yes.

"Yes."

"Maybe it'll be easier for you out there."

I didn't tell Charlie that I awaited finding out much like I had the oncoming wave of traffic on my mental Fifth Avenue.

CHAPTER TEN

My Connecticut place had once been an outbuilding of a grand estate that has since disappeared, leaving my cottage the only vestige of what once was there. It was made of native stone and had an appealing gabled roof, its original tiny windows having been replaced with generous ones that let in copious light. The grounds were lush with a smorgasbord of trees, white birch, sassafras, pine, chestnut, weeping willow, maple, crab apple, cherry, fir, dogwood, and quince, and rhododendron bushes. There was a wide flagstone terrace overlooking a spacious lawn that featured a reflecting pool with a pair of spouting flamingoes and a family of koi that had prospered over the years. A small stone fence topped by anti-deer netting encircled the property.

My hope that the Bonnet syndrome would not extend its dragnet to this heavenly retreat was quickly dispelled. To my eyes, the modest fence was now a huge wall of decaying, slotted wood that blocked my exquisite view. The pool's surface was covered with feathery wood chips and the cottage's windows were clouded, the bathroom abused just as it was in

New York. Altogether, a thorough despoiling of this blessed place.

There was also this peculiar restaurant affliction: there were many excellent dining places near me that I liked to frequent with Charlie and Lydia and other friends. That weekend, I managed to go to more than one of these places without incident, but invariably, on the drive from the restaurant back to my place, the road was encased with very high continuous structures of antique wood that rose above the trees and local buildings. These dark syndrome buildings had a medieval look, with windows and indented balconies but no sign of habitation. Decidedly spooky. And at times, whether I was in an Uber or in Charlie's car, there would be mysterious lights hovering above outside the windows, and the perfectly smooth asphalt road would suddenly become bumpy and torn up, or covered with what looked like the shattered residue of a hurricane. That is what I saw; the driver of course experienced none of it.

As if making sure its control resonated with me, the Bonnet syndrome took me on an extended hallucination. As usual there was no preamble, no warning. I found myself lying on my back on a street that was busy with promenading people. They were walking together in twos, threes, fours, dressed colorfully, some in military uniforms with bright medals on their chest, uniforms that were unlike any I had ever seen. There were mailmen, bus drivers, politicians, fishermen, mothers pushing baby buggies, doctors, nurses: a panorama of city people. They all walked past me paying me no attention. As the ones in uniform walked by, I put my arm up from the ground and called out, "Please give me a hand," but it got no response other than a few sideways looks.

As for me, I think I did want assistance, but at the same

time I was fascinated by what I regarded as Syndrome City. Many of the pedestrians were identical twosomes, three-somes, and foursomes of an exactness that defied explanation. This also applied to the four perfectly replicated horses pulling a wagon, to the two policemen on the corner, to the three dogs on a leash. I was also mesmerized by the absolute silence. No automobile horns, no streetcar clangs, no barking, no voices—in fact, no city sounds.

I implored cops, big men in butcher's aprons, priests, anyone who looked likely to "give me a hand," extending my arms to them, but although a few stopped to look at me like I was a zoo animal, they all moved on, except for a mailman who had his pouch on his shoulder. It took him a while to make up his mind but finally he reached down to my eager hand and grasped it. I responded, but there was nothing there, no substance whatsoever.

The mailman pulled his arm away as three men wearing gold uniforms of some sort surrounded him. They concentrated their looks on him, but even though their lips and hands weren't moving, they were obviously chastising him in some way for trying to help me, a human who, like all humans, was considered unacceptable and out of bounds.

At this point I decided to impose my brain on this hallucinatory distortion. I deliberately heard echoes of Dr. Brevoro's exhortations and I tried to overcome my acceptance of what this hallucination dictated by straining to stand up and get on my feet. But an inner voice asked me where I could go, what would I do, and, feeling a kind of hypnotic restraint, I abandoned my self-actualizing urge and succumbed to the grip of the syndrome.

I was moved around what I can only refer to as "their city." I was placed in their streetcars, but I couldn't tell if fares were being paid as passengers got on and off. There were little lakes everywhere with small paddleboats occupied by two or three people, who seemed to revel in them. All these boats had colored banners flying above their sterns, and they appeared to enjoy racing each other.

There were large ice-skating rinks populated with very adept skaters, and fields where games were in progress, but I didn't recognize any of them as related to any I had ever seen or heard about. We passed one busy windowless building that had guards with swords outside, probably a jail. An impressive giant circus was in progress, funny clowns galore and beautiful horses adroitly performing with bespangled riders doing dangerous bareback routines at full speed. There were complicated high aerial acts featuring ten trapezes manned by twenty aerialists doing perilous turns.

Suddenly, I found myself catapulted up the ladder to the aerial platform, and pushed to the end of the take-off platform as a trapeze was coming at me. I looked down fearfully at the ground far below—no safety net—but was given no chance to act before I was pushed forward into space to connect with the hands of an approaching trapeze artist. I grabbed them, but the outstretched hands had no substance, nothing to hold on to, and I flew past them, tumbling in space and landing in my bed in Connecticut, aware that I was screaming in protest.

"It's haunted me all week," I told Dr. Brevoro. "I take it to bed with me, relive it while I eat, trying to make sense of my behavior."

"Did you try to convince yourself it was just your haunted brain playing tricks?"

"Yes . . . somewhat, especially when I was thrown in the midst of the trapeze aerialists. But I was refuted by a kind of paralyzing lethargy, as if I'd been hypnotized."

"Would you say you were enjoying what was happening to you? None of this was actually threatening, was it?"

"Not really, there were no monsters or ugly disagreeable characters . . ."

"But they wouldn't give you a hand . . ."

"Well, to tell the truth, it was like when I tried to push those children out of my bedroom and found that there was nothing there to push. But still I regarded them as children, so expertly presented were they. So it was with these people on parade, on the barges, in the shops. The totally real way they behaved, their realistic, believable, authentic existence, refuted the scolding of my brain to the extent that I was fascinated by them."

I dropped forward, my head in my hands—it was a humiliating relief to finally be able to air my thoughts to a sympathetic ear.

"It is almost how a great novel introduces characters who remain very real long after you've finished reading the book," I said. "But the difference here is, of course, that I am propelled into the action and must contend with these upsetting characters who can thrust themselves on me anytime, anyplace they desire, thereby disrupting my existence. It seems foolish now, but when this all started I briefly had this fantasy the syndrome would break through my writer's block—free ideas for life, right? But instead my head feels befuddled all the time and I can't even *imagine* being able to write. I'm just choked all the time by fearfulness about the next syndrome attack."

"Can you recall your emotions when they raised you up

to the aerial platform high above the ground and you saw no safety net below?"

"At first I thought it was a bluff to scare me, but when I felt that push on my back that catapulted me off the platform into open space, I screamed and felt the certainty of death."

"So this was not the muted reaction you had to the replicated people?"

"Yes. I was totally absorbed in the trapeze. I had surrendered my identity. I was there in that underground city—no matter that there was no such city or people or trapeze—I bought it hook, line, and sinker. So is that my fate?"

"Perhaps it would help you if I shared with you the syndrome incidents my patients have accepted into their everyday lives." He opened his notebook. "Patient one: a giant blue and gray moth, bigger than a 747, comes flapping at her, the wings big enough to suffocate her, and at the last second the moth elevates over her head and zooms off, leaving her collapsed on the ground from her fright. Patient two: dead of night, band of grotesquely clothed men infiltrates her bedroom wall and while whistling settles down on her bed, staring closely into her face, causing her to dive under the covers, and by the time she finally emerges two hours later they have disappeared. Patient three: 'It was a bright moonlit night, I was sitting in my garden when a huge herd of buffalo came roaring through the fence, headed my way. I did not try to run, just froze, and the beasts split around me. Despite knowing they were unreal syndrome buffalo, I still feared they'd trample me, and I covered my face with my arms.' Patient four: can see pages of music with complete scores, notes, clefs, accents, rests, but when she tried to play them it turned out they were complete fakes, unplayable, and made no musical sense whatsoever.

"Like you, these people must live with their Bonnet syndrome, as do many others like them, although the syndrome threatens to intrude into their normal lives and diminish them. But unlike you, they no longer try to combat them. They have accommodated them in their lives, and that's what you must do to get the most out of your life now. You can't do anything to stop syndrome kids from showing up for television. You *can* do something about your attitude, and by accepting them, you may discourage them from appearing at all—or at least as often. None of my patients have been subjected to personal assaults the way you have. You can only hope that events as physical as being trapped in that crate and flying through the air cease to be the norm."

"God knows, do I. You once mentioned there was a medicine that worked somewhat on a patient and I thought I should try it; what have I got to lose?"

"Why not? However, none of my patients were helped—although one got better for a short while—and a few complained of side effects." He started to write out a prescription. "It's called quetiapine." He tore a page off his pad and gave it to me. "It may slow things down a bit. I really think you will only help yourself if you can change your attitude and stop trying to resist the forces of the Bonnet syndrome."

The first order of business had to be giving up my single practice and bringing in a new attorney to backstop me. I visited Shirley Fiske, an old friend from law school who had gone on to become the dean at Cardozo law school, to ask her if she might suggest a young lawyer who would be a fit for my practice. She happened to have recently been visited by a former student who had gone to Paris after graduation to get a PhD in French literature and now, four years later, was back and wanting to know if she might be aware of a law firm where she might find an interesting opening.

"She'd be perfect for you, Chet: graduated second in her class, article editor of our law journal, fine personality. What do you say?"

"I'd certainly like to meet her."

"She left me her phone number . . ." She fished around in a desk drawer until she located it. "Yes, Lois Lowell, yes, here you are. She's the first in her Georgia family to go to university. I would have put her on the faculty if I had the opening."

I had lunch with Lois at the Trattoria Dell'Arte, and she was everything and more than Shirley had proffered. We settled on the details of her affiliation before espresso arrived, and she came back with me to the office. I planned to tell her about my Bonnet syndrome, but, I decided, another time. I was, in a sense, self-conscious about my condition, and I didn't feel like putting myself on exhibit. It made me feel, well, I guess you'd say "damaged," not able to maintain myself. Not a good perch for a boss to occupy.

Lois exuded self-confidence. She seemed genuinely pleased with the nature of my practice, now hers, and she thrust herself into learning as much about the intimate aspects of how the publishing business intersected with the law as she could.

With this addition of another qualified lawyer to back me up, I felt less vulnerable to syndrome interference. To further solidify my existence under the syndrome threat, I had alarms installed in both my New York apartment and my Connecticut cottage. The syndrome activities at night had become more insistent and penetrating and depressing. There were times in the pitch-dark quiet of the silent night when the syndrome activity suddenly erupted and fear rode up my chest. To have a button that connected me to the local police was reassuring, if only to be used with severe restraint.

I did eventually inform Lois about my syndrome, and her youthful reaction was, "If it was me, I'd concentrate on what about them I could find positive and good for a laugh."

"If only it would be as simple as that. I just want you to know because I may need you to cover for me if the occasion arises."

"I plan to research this Bonnet syndrome and learn as much as I can about it. I'll discuss it with you along the way."

"I'd rather not, Lois. The more I talk about it, the more it frazzles me. But, yes, I hope you do read up on it."

In the weeks that followed I did my damnedest not to be negative toward whatever the syndrome unleashed, but I wasn't very good at it. I was constantly trying to devise methods to turn away the assailers. I moved my furniture around in my New York apartment, blocking the area where the children would crowd around to watch television. When the road in Connecticut was invariably beset with all those medieval buildings and dilapidated neighborhoods only seen by me, I'd shut my eyes and try not to be irritated by looking at them. But even with my eyes shut, the syndromers managed to throw repulsive visions into my brain.

But for the most part I made myself go along with the indignations hurled at me. Three strutting pigeons on the balcony of my New York apartment turned into three dancing squirrels when I went out on the balcony, then the squirrels turned into three large rats that ran around chasing each other before floating off the balcony and disappearing into the sky. Another time, vines thick with sunflowers began to entwine themselves all over the balcony and choke the view when I was sitting in a chair.

When I was in my New York apartment, syndrome activity was incessant. Geraniums would fill the bathtub, but when I got in, there were no plants, though the impression of the plants would appear on my body. One night I awoke with a start to find three hideous faces looking into mine, barbarous faces of villainous men, snarling, ferocious, bloody. I howled and pulled the covers over my head, blocking out the sight of them. I continued my protesting with my eyes covered and yearned for a panic button on the headboard that would give me a sense of protection but that I would probably never give in to.

And so it went. However I tried, I couldn't make any real headway toward reforming my attitude toward the constant syndrome obscenities. To be awakened from a deep sleep with the ghoulish faces of three fiends hanging over you, peering into your eyes, is not conducive to saying, "Hiya, chaps, glad to see you."

I tried to induce myself to start writing a new addition to my detective series but I still hadn't regained my ability to—ouch—see things from Honeywell's perspective.

At least my practice was running smoothly enough. While I was still at a loss for how to prepare for trial in the Tee case, the intrusions had not affected my legal judgment and therefore my clients could still rely upon me to offer sagacious pearls of legal wisdom, such as "Don't put Mickey Mouse on your book cover if you don't want Disney to sue you." Lois had avidly devoted herself to studying and taking courses in copyright, defamation, right of publicity, and all the rest of what I call "publication law." She had an enchanting personality and worked well with some of the journalists who were my clients. I would sometimes brave lunch with Lois, and she handled the annoying vicissitudes of my syndrome assaults with ease.

As Doc Brevoro had predicted, the quetiapine, like all the other attempted remedies, had no effect on the stings of the syndrome thrown at me. I tried to maintain the optimism he counseled was necessary to thrive beneath the yoke of the Bonnet, but I found myself nagged by a perceptible decline in my enjoyment of the overall life I was now living, focused as it was entirely around a disease that accepts no cure.

CHAPTER ELEVEN

The one constant that had always served me well was my deep friendship with Charlie. Aware of my gradual withdrawal from social activity, he made sure we dined often, especially in the country, and that we had lunch every Wednesday in New York. When we lunched alone he always made a point of talking about my fears and despondencies. He did it in such a fraternal way that I looked forward to the times I could see him and discharge some of my troubles and menacing thoughts into his safekeeping, helping me back to a positive attitude.

So it was on my way to have my weekly lunch with Charlie at Mykonos that I found myself on the corner of Fifty-Ninth and Madison, waiting—not without anxiety, considering past syndrome visits—for the "Walk" light to appear. About a dozen of us were pressed close together as we stepped off the curb and hurried to beat the countdown. However, halfway across, a woman walking beside me stumbled. To keep from falling, she grabbed my sleeve. Instinctively, I tried to help her, but she pitched forward, ripping my sleeve from my suit coat as she fell forcefully onto the road, striking her head. Blood started to run down her face as she lay motionless, unconscious, my sleeve clasped in one of her hands. For a moment I was unsure whether any of this was real, but then two men and a woman broke away from the crowd and stayed with me to help wave off the oncoming cars and buses. The woman called 911. The two men wanted to move the fallen woman out of the traffic and to the sidewalk, but I told them that with a head injury we'd better leave her as she was until the ambulance arrived. New York drivers being what they are, they jockeyed each other as close as possible to us, on top of which there were bicycles, buses, trucks, pedicabs, electric scooters, and God knows what else threatening us in a decidedly unballetic fashion. One of the men was wearing a topcoat, and he took it off and covered the stricken woman with it. As far as I could tell she was a rather well-dressed, attractive young woman, but I was too occupied with the unruly traffic to actually concentrate on her.

An ambulance from Lenox Hill Hospital, its siren clearing the way, parked diagonally in front of us, blocking off the immediate traffic. A squad car with two cops pulled up and funneled all traffic into a single lane until the unconscious woman could be removed. The ambulance driver and the technician inside first attended to the woman's bleeding forehead, and when it was stanched, they brought a stretcher from the ambulance and very carefully wrapped a neck brace around her throat and straightened out her body. They slowly edged her onto the stretcher and took her into the ambulance. One of the police came over to me.

"You with the woman?"

"No. We were in a group crossing and she grabbed on to my sleeve to keep from falling."

"Then you don't know her?"

"No, not at all."

He asked the other two men and the woman, but they didn't know her either.

He came back to me. "You see her handbag?"

"I think I did, lying on the ground over there when she first fell."

"But you didn't pick it up?"

"No. Too busy with the traffic."

"Well, it's not here. You mind coming to the hospital? We've got to fill out a report, and we need your statement."

The ambulance attendants had carried the woman from the street and into the ambulance and secured her. I took off my one-armed suit coat and got in the ambulance with the attendant. The driver closed the back doors on his way to the driver's seat and put the ambulance in motion along with its siren. The squad car led the way to the hospital, its own siren going full blast.

The attendant covered the woman with a blanket. He picked up a phone that hung on the side of the ambulance and dialed a number. "Emergency Department," he said, and told someone his ambulance, number thirty-six, was bringing in an unconscious woman with bleeding head trauma.

When we arrived at the hospital there was a team waiting for her, headed by the chief emergency physician. The woman was still unconscious. New dressings were applied to her forehead, which had not completely stopped bleeding. Another doctor appeared, identified on his white jacket as Dr. E. R. MacIntire, Neurology. He examined the woman's forehead and raised her eyelids to inspect her eyes.

"Did she fall on her head?" he asked.

"Yes," I said, "in the street."

"All right, let's get a quick CAT scan. There may be internal bleeding in the brain. Let's step on it."

The cop came to get my statement about what had happened. I asked him about the woman's identity.

"Don't have it," he said. "We've searched the corner wire baskets for her purse, but it's not there. Snatchers usually pocket the money, throw the handbag away. Not this time. Hopefully she'll come out of it soon and then we can ask *her*."

I went into the emergency waiting room and called Charlie on my cell to explain why I had missed lunch, and apologized.

"Well, at last a girl finally fell for you."

"She's a mystery girl."

"How so?"

"Someone stole her handbag after she fell and there's no way to identify her."

"Expensive shoes and dress?"

"No, not really."

"What did she look like?"

"Couldn't tell. Her hair was sort of stuck to her face, plus the bandage and some street dirt."

"Well, don't worry, someone will report her missing—always do."

"I hope she keeps my sleeve, that was a favorite suit."

I had a very busy afternoon working with an editor who was questioning the way some people were depicted in a book he was publishing—the autobiography of a Hall of Fame baseball superstar who had a scurvy side to him and had depicted some people in a potentially libelous manner.

It was seven o'clock when we finally, with Lois's help, finished, and as I was locking up I found myself thinking about the nameless woman and her fate. That she had grabbed my sleeve somehow in a funny way tied our fates, so I took a cab to Lenox Hill to see how she was doing (and, incidentally, to retrieve my sleeve).

I intercepted an obliging nurse who was on the way out of the ER. She said there had been no change in the woman's condition—that she had not regained consciousness and no one had shown up to identify her.

The following day I stopped by the hospital on my way home from lunch with a client, and this time I fortunately saw Dr. MacIntire in the corridor.

"She is still unconscious but not showing any of the usual causes, like a fracture or swelling of the brain or anything else that we can identify. You don't know who she is, do you?"

"No, just happened to be there when she fell."

"And no one was with her?"

"No one I saw."

"I can tell you all her vital signs are relatively normal. We've taken her off everything—hasn't seemed to make any difference. And all the things we've done to restore consciousness also seem to have had no effect on her."

I left again, curiosity and anxiety unabated. I was much more concerned about this mystery woman than I should have been. Why? Maybe it was that when she started to fall and clutched at me, I failed to grab her and keep her from falling—a far-fetched justification for a peculiar kind of guilt I couldn't explain.

CHAPTER TWELVE

On the third day of the mystery woman's incarceration, I again went to the hospital to check on her status and to my surprise found that she was no longer in the Emergency Department. I checked at the information desk and discovered that she had been moved to a step-down unit, which meant that she had improved, probably regained consciousness.

When I reached her location, there was a man in a black suit with a briefcase talking loudly to a woman, obviously my mystery woman, who was in bed. Her forehead was bandaged and she wore a heavy hospital robe. She was conscious.

"Madame," the man was saying, "just sign this permission for me to represent you against the city and I guarantee you from a hundred thou on up. I'm very well connected at city hall."

He was thrusting a pen with a document at her.

The woman said, "No."

I stepped into the room and approached the man. "Who are you?"

He proffered me his embossed card: *Harlan Fitzheimer,* and underneath that, *Attorney at Law.*

"I can get a hundred thou for a fall with a bruise, a hundred fifty on up if there's blood. This one plus unconscious can easy go double."

He was a short ambulance chaser; I was looking down on him from six foot two. "Fitzheimer," I said, "you hear what the lady said?"

"Yes, but she's still a little crackers from her fall in that pothole."

"She said no, right?"

"Yes, but listen, I can get you three—"

"Fitzheimer, no is no, there was no pothole, put your pen and paper in your briefcase and get your skinny ass out of here."

"But I—"

"Now."

"But—"

"Right! Now!"

I moved close to him. He opened his briefcase, tossed in the paper and pen, and snapped it shut.

"If she changes her mind—"

"Don't hold your breath."

He left.

I went to the bed. Her face was buried in the covers. She said, "Thank you so much," her soft voice muffled. "Who are you?"

"Chet Tremaine. I was walking beside you when you fell on the street."

Three people came sweeping into the room, two doctors and a nurse. One doctor was the emergency room MD I had previously spoken to. The doctors went directly to the bed to talk to the woman, while the nurse came over to me and asked me to leave. I wrote my name and phone number on a slip of paper I took from my pocket and asked her to give it to the patient. Below my contact information I had written: "Please call me at your convenience about my sleeve. Thanks."

I thought about my mystery woman several times that week, disappointed I hadn't heard from her but nevertheless still curious about her. However, after over a week passed without a phone call, I conceded she'd unfortunately remain a mystery to me.

But then the call did come. Even after barely having heard her speak, I recognized her voice, her soft British accent. "Hello, is this Mr. Tremaine?"

"Yes."

She told me what I already knew—that she was the woman from the hospital—and introduced herself as Emma Vicky. "Sorry I am delayed getting in touch with you but that bloody fall has certainly slowed me down."

"You certainly sound pretty all right for someone who took a spill like that."

"They told me I grabbed at you to try to keep from banging down."

"The whole bunch of us pedestrians got tangled up . . ."

"I have no memory of any of it, but I do have your sleeve. It looks like it might be able to find its way back to your coat. Would you like to come by for a drink and a thank-you to reclaim it? I am pretty much confined for the time being."

Despite my worries about venturing out with the syndrome stalking me, I said I would. She gave me her address on Gramercy Square, which happens to be one of my favorite

New York neighborhoods, a private locked little park surrounded by distinguished apartments and town houses that own the coveted keys. Her lilting laugh held the promise of someone out of the ordinary.

The Emma Vicky who answered the bell was a distant cry from the begrimed street refugee I had seen in the ambulance. I stood there at her door, transfixed, with a bottle of chilled Tavel rosé in a silver carton under my arm and my good eye assessing her high cheekbones, deep-set eyes, thick blond hair held high in a ponytail, and tender smile.

"Come in, come in. I thought you'd be older."

I handed her the wine. "I think we should drink to your recovery—three days completely out of it seems pretty ominous. You baffled all the specialty doctors."

She took the Tavel out of its carton, handed it to me with an opener, and set two wineglasses on a coffee table in front of a patterned couch. The view from her living room was directly over several flowering dogwoods in the secluded park. As far as I could tell, the apartment was a small one-bedroom with a spare room and a full, sunny kitchen. I poured the wine and proffered a toast: "May good health now overtake you."

We sipped appreciatively. "So tell me," I asked, "those days in the hospital when you were unconscious and nobody showed up to claim you . . ."

"Did you come by?"

"Yes, I had to keep an eye on you—you were the keeper of my sleeve, weren't you?"

She laughed.

"No husband, relatives, close friends, nobody?"

"Nope. In fact, I'm an actress without a stage."

"Meaning?"

"Actually I'm a British actress who came here with a touring group from the London stage to perform in cities and universities in repertory, in *The Cherry Orchard*, *A Streetcar Named Desire*, and *A Midsummer Night's Dream*."

"I'll wager you played Stella."

"We had a splendid run. I fell in love with Americans. But just before our farewell performances in Brooklyn, my world came crashing down. A totally destructive tsunami that came with no warning, none whatsoever . . ." She pulled up with a self-conscious shrug. I freshened our wine. Her eyes were closed as, reminiscing, she took a sip. "I haven't . . ." She stopped. "You mind if I go off the subject?"

"Please don't. I'd really like to hear . . ."

"I rarely mention it to anyone. I have to keep myself from myself."

"Might help you deal with it."

"Not likely. I have something you've probably never heard of . . . and neither have most other people, including MDs. It's called Ménière's disease."

"You're right—sounds like a sauce."

She laughed. "You're right. Filet of sole meunière. No, this Ménière's is named after the French doctor who discovered it more than a century ago. Quite rare, a constant threat, night and day, incurable but not lethal. How's that for a tantalizing combination?"

I nearly choked on my wine hearing this echoing description of my own affliction.

She stood up. "Let's skip my miserable miseries. There's lots livelier things to talk about. Excuse me while I rustle up a few nibbles." She went into the kitchen.

I shook my head in disbelief. Two little-known afflictions discovered long ago by a couple of Europeans still afflicting us with no cure in sight. Dr. Ménière, meet Dr. Bonnet.

Yet I decided to keep my syndrome to myself for the time being. I was intrigued with this appealing sleeve grabber and I didn't want to intrude with my own peculiar situation.

She returned with a platter of cheeses—camembert, brie, gorgonzola—crackers, fresh dates, two plates, and a cheese knife. She prepared an assortment on each plate and we resumed our position on the couch. To my consternation, as I placed a sliver of brie on a cracker, everything on my plate became covered with Bonnet's sprigs of fake greenery. She could not see them, of course; I ate the cheese, sprigs, cracker, and all.

"You were about to tell me . . . ," I said.

"Well, yes, as I said, it was the night before our final performance when it happened without warning, no warning at all, just a violent, abrupt, frightening awakening, alone in a hotel room that was whirling around and around like a ride gone out of control in an amusement park, my ears deafened by a roaring wind, the only telephone on the other side of the room, but how to reach it? Trying to get out of bed, my balance deserted me and I collapsed headfirst onto the carpet. I couldn't raise my head, my face was buried in the carpet, but using my arms I managed to pull and push my body inch by tortured inch across the carpet to the telephone. I was totally incoherent but I somehow reached someone to call for help. I could barely form words. Luckily I made myself understood. Then days and weeks of all kinds of testing, frustrated doctors unable to isolate what had brought me down. Finally—finally!—they identified that this sudden attack was caused by a well-disguised Ménière's—in doctor's talk, epidemic rotational vertigo—you're probably not interested in all this stuff . . ."

"Yes I am. *Very* interested! Please go on . . ."

"Well, it's your whole head spinning and a roaring, buzzing, ringing sound in the inner ear, but it's not known what causes it, only that it attacks without warning and can wreck the balance of its victims. In the year that followed that first attack I was not able to take care of myself, had to have a full-time nurse by my side day and night. All the repertory players, the director, the staff, had to return to England and I was on my own, flat on me arse. Luckily I had actors' insurance that covered me. A woman at the British embassy in New York City befriended me, found me this apartment and the help I needed. And I sure needed it. I was black and blue and yellow and green all over from getting thrown down and around by the damn vertigo."

"What about your family? Your mother and father?"

"Had no father—disappeared, or maybe didn't appear at all. Never got that straight. Anyway, Mom had to raise me on her own. She and her friend Molly Wicker, also husbandless, started a bridal shop, Here Comes the Bride, in London, and made a great go of it, put me through university and a three-year enrollment in the Royal Academy."

"But she didn't come to help you?"

Emma was staring at the wall.

I repeated the question.

"No. I lost her. Brides' gowns is a seasonal business and Mom was too busy to have the mastectomy she needed, and in the end it was just too late when she finally tried to take care of it. Molly still runs Bride and I get a share, but when I think what Mom sacrificed so that I could act . . . and the irony is that she put off her life so I could perform, and now I can't act at all."

"Why not?"

"Because my vertigo could kick in when I was emoting in the middle of a scene. Mary Queen of Scots drunk as a dancing bear. Specialists ran a gazillion tests." She opened a drawer, took out a list, which she read from: "Audiometric examination of my ears; an ENG to measure my balance; ECOG measuring the inner ear; ABR brain-stem tests of my hearing, nerves, and brain paths. These tests and others produced no clue, nothing as to what had caused my condition, nor did they suggest any treatment to correct it or even make it less explosive. My life was acutely restricted. Any motion could trigger a severe fall, so I couldn't travel at all; even a taxi ride could be too much of a risk. Since there is no known cure for Ménière's, I had to abandon even the hope of ever acting again. My physician said that most victims would not risk a sudden attack, which could be catastrophic, and as a result never traveled anywhere or ventured very far from their homes. This was Van Gogh's affliction," she said, "and it was the tinnitus in his ears that drove him to cut off one of them. My physician said he hoped I wouldn't try to imitate him."

I asked her if she wasn't supposed to go anywhere alone, how come she had been crossing that street by herself when she fell.

"Well, the first year after that initial fall I was horrified. I was a head-twirling, mind-bending, staggering veggie, but Dorothy Plum, the British embassy woman, was a godsend. She came to see me quite often, and so did a professor from New York University who taught Shakespeare and had seen me in *Midsummer*. Their lively visits and my own determination began to lift me from the snake pit, and by the end of the second year I had recovered somewhat. Not so whirly, not so wobbly. On my last birthday I got myself by the scruff of my neck (which is quite a contortion), stood myself in front of that mirror over there, and said, 'Okay, Emma, okay, what'll it be? Keep yourself in purgatory for the rest of your life or try to pick up and restore some of the pieces?' So . . . one thing I did was search for any new hope. I discovered one medicine widely used with some success in Europe, but not approved by the FDA and not available here. My doctor was able to get it for me and it's cut down a bit on the frequency of the whirlies and the somersaults, but I still need someone to keep an eye on me if I venture out. I have also discovered there is a prescription stick-it-on to plaster behind your ear before flying that can possibly keep you from collapsing in flight. I haven't tested it, of course, but the point is that's a little hope."

"But when you fell, why were you alone?"

"Well, it was like this: A new place has opened in the city—I think it's run by one of the hospitals—with a radical treatment for Ménière's people like me. You go three times a week and it's a tough workout—they put me on a machine that shakes me violently side to side, up and down, spins me, stuff like that. Don't know if it will really help but I'm going to try everything. I sure as sour apples am not going to surrender. Not me! So . . . I signed up but had to figure out how I could get someone to cover me three times a week, wait thirty minutes, and take me back. Know who I got? A nice young woman who walks a posse of dogs she picks up in this block, and now she accompanies me like I'm a golden retriever."

"Do you have a collar and a leash?"

She barked and we both laughed.

"But on the day we . . . met, sort of, she called in sick and I thought I was ready to go on my own. I had been occasionally going alone to a bench in the park right across the street armed with my doorman's whistle, you see. And until my fall with you, I was doing just fine, but then when we were crossing, someone behind me pushed me a little and that's what caused my Ménière's eruption and my head bang, not a pothole."

I poured the last of the wine. "You are certainly doing your damnedest to escape your Ménière's," I said, "and this prison, nice as it is."

"Luckily there are two or three restaurants near here who deliver, and I also have frozen foods that I order online to make in my microwave. I can't do any real cooking since I'm not allowed to risk the gas flames of the stove when I might have an eruption, but Dorothy Plum of the embassy often comes bringing dinner and good conversation. She's like a godsend mother. I've not yet risked going to a restaurant but there's a bright spot: Dorothy has induced a man she knows who runs an advertising agency to try my British accent for a voice-over commercial for a London line of beauty products. I've got a little recording setup here and so far there's only been one time I've had to delay briefly because of a bit of the whirlies . . . oh my, I've run on much too long, haven't I? That's because you're such a really, really good listener."

"That's because I'm hearing for the first time about your incurable Ménière's whirly-whirlies and what they've done to you, which matches my incurable Bonnet syndrome and what it's done to me."

"What? What! You're kidding, you're pulling my leg, aren't you?"

"You've never heard of Charles Bonnet syndrome, have you?"

"No. Is it contagious?"

"Not at all. What about Ménière's?"

"Nope. Who are you? You feel like someone . . . I don't know . . . someone I've known and yet . . . are you married?"

"No. You?"

"No. Divorced?"

"No. You?"

"No. Engaged?"

"No. Was but Bonnet put an end to it. You?"

"Same here. Said he was afraid I wouldn't have children."

"Pity."

"Not really since it made me realize he was a bloody stiff banker and I was well out of it." The telephone rang. "Do you mind? I get so few, can't afford to miss any."

"Go right ahead."

"Oh, hello, Dorothy. Guess who's here—the chap who guarded me when I bonkered in the street . . . yes, the one with the sleeve."

Emma had a bubbly exchange from which I gathered Dorothy was apologizing for not being able to come for dinner this evening because of an unexpected crisis at the embassy. Emma, understandably, graciously excused her, and they proceeded to chat about future plans.

I was sitting there, half listening to her end of the conversation—mostly just the tone and rhythm of her voice—when I realized to my surprise that I was smiling to myself. I resettled my expression: I felt totally unprepared for this little intrusion in my life, an upset of my determination to accept the domination of Bonnet syndrome.

"Poor Dorothy," Emma said as she rejoined me, "has a night call at her embassy. She was supposed to come for dinner."

"May I fill in?" I was surprised by these aggressive words coming spontaneously from me.

"You're free? Wonderful. There's a restaurant nearby that has an authentic Sicilian wood-burning oven and delivers a sensational Vesuvian pizza that flows down you like hot lava. Are you game for that? I have a Valpolicella red that'll fan the fires. What do you say?"

"I say you're rescuing me from having a Stouffer's lasagna out of my microwave."

"You know, all this time I haven't heard a word about you. Just me, me, me."

"Well, hearing those incredible things about you, you, you was certainly fascinating."

And that's how the evening began. She was intrigued with the literary nature of my law practice, wanting to hear about some of the dramatic cases. We were interrupted by the arrival of the Vesuvian pizza, but then I got around to the effects of my right eye's being blinded on a tennis court . . .

"So, Chet, unhappily we do have something in common—we can't drive, because I know the danger of spinning out at the wheel and you may get blindsided by traffic on your right."

When I got around to telling her about some of the more dramatic ordeals I had undergone in my syndrome episodes, she couldn't get enough of them. But I finally called it quits. "I will have to pull down the curtain and save more for another time."

"Oh, yes, please! What about tomorrow? Can you tolerate me two days in a row?"

The word *yes!* stuck in my throat. I wanted to give voice to it so badly; I wanted to promise tomorrow, and the day after, and the day after that. But she'd only heard about the Bonnet; she hadn't experienced it. My brain—the regular old organ, sans syndrome—threw up an image of lovely young Emma Vicky chained up in a crate beside me . . . No. I couldn't do that to her.

"I'm afraid I'm busy tomorrow. But maybe soon . . . I'll call you."

I'm not sure what she read in my expression, but she smiled bravely in the face of it and began to pack up the cheeses. I swiftly moved to help, putting the Vesuvian remains in the pizza box. With our arms full of all this plus the empty wine bottles and glasses, we started toward the kitchen, but as she stepped from the living room carpet onto the kitchen floor she began to wobble. Then with a piercing "Oh, no!" she stumbled, giving up her cargo. I let go of mine and made an attempt to keep her from falling by grabbing her arm to keep her upright, but the momentum caused our feet to get tangled. I landed on a pancaked gorgonzola and Emma was sprawled in the midst of a sea of crumbled crackers.

For a moment, we were both silent aside from a few startled, breathless pants. Then I scooped the gorgonzola covering my backside with a finger and plunged it in my mouth, and she dribbled a handful of crackers in hers. We took a look at each other and simultaneously began to laugh: no ordinary twitter but a laugh that came from the belly on up, a laugh fueled by the ridiculous nature of our fates. Tears came with the laughter and I pulled out my handkerchief, tore it in two, pitched a half to her. We wiped our eyes and blew our noses and let our laughter slowly play itself out.

We sat facing each other among the detritus like two kids in a sandbox.

I asked, "Do you sometimes wind up wiped out like this when you're alone?"

"Sometimes."

"What if you get injured—like turn your ankle and it's really hard to get up? Maybe impossible?"

She pulled a cord from around her neck that had a device on the end of it. "I'd press this button that has a helping voice on the end of it that connects to the concierge desk in the lobby, as well as to a nearby nurses' station."

"You mean a button like this?" I asked, pulling out an identical device from my pocket. "You're not the only one who needs help. Like me sometimes after a killer syndrome episode. But they only work indoors. Outside you have to use your cell phone, and I suggest you add my number to your contacts. Just call out my name, tell me where you are, and I'll be there for you."

I did not suggest she reciprocate. Unlike Emma, I couldn't be helped.

"I can't believe it!" Emma was still releasing gasps of breathless laughter. "Both of us with the same needy buttons. You stuck with your crazies, me whirling with mine. But no! We can't let them bury us. Do you hear?"

Instead of answering, I got up and, putting my hands under her arms, helped her to her feet. She smiled up at me, a luminous smile that elicited a contagious response from me.

Just then, a flow of syndrome people pranced into the room: stylishly outfitted men wearing hats and neckties, women with designer dresses and handbags. They clustered around us, looking us over intently. Their heady gazes seemed to declare that I was foolish to think I could even have one evening alone with Emma. I waved a hostile arm at them. "All right, get out, get out of here," I commanded in a crisp voice. As usual they paid no attention. Emma began to pick up the fallen cheeses and shattered glass, but she was unsteady and started to sway, so I caught her again and this time kept her from falling.

"Oh, thanks. Could you help me to the bedroom?"

She took off her shoes and with my help lay down on the bed.

"Do you need to call someone?"

"No. I have pills for this." She opened the night table drawer and took out a bottle. "A couple of these and a good night's sleep will be just fine."

"Do you need anything else?"

"No, thanks. You were a lovely help."

I passed her the glass of water from the nightstand. She took it, her cool fingers lingering for a moment on mine.

"Do call," she said. "When you can."

Feeling awkward, I kissed her hand and left.

The syndrome people were all gone.

CHAPTER THIRTEEN

Back at my apartment, I remained dizzied from the long encounter with Emma: the easy way we had bared ourselves; our detailed confessions; my eagerness to reach out to her, but to what end?

I made myself a tidy drink and immersed myself in watching the flow of traffic thirty-seven floors below, a torrent of red glowing taillights moving in one direction and streaming white headlights in the other. I had to admit leaving Emma like that with my failure of a promise and a few polite words was disappointing. I should have shown some warmth in my good night, something to indicate how attractive she was to me, how much I wished things could be different. Even though I knew it to be impossible.

And to further drive home that point, that night the Bonnet syndrome reasserted itself. I closed my eyes against the burning sting of my predicament and found myself in a vast decorated space dominated by a mammoth Morpheus statue and filled with hundreds of identical beds with uniform sheets, pillows, and blankets, all in orderly arrangement.

I was in one of the beds, which had a high metal filigreed barrier on each side that could be raised or lowered. I was lying on my back, head on a pillow, covered by a white blanket. Mine was the only bed that was occupied. The aisles between the beds were filled with roving syndromers, nightclothes draped over their arms, inspecting the beds. As they passed mine, I reached up and called out, "Give me a hand," but they didn't even look my way.

The giant Morpheus suddenly exuded a bright blue canopy as a band of regal white horses came in, ridden in formation by white-clad horsemen who with jeweled batons induced the circling sleep-clad syndromers to enter the beds, one after the other. In no time all the beds were filled and colored lights with beautiful patterns began to play over our heads. As the colored lights started to fade and complete darkness replaced them, the horsemen activated torches and rode among the beds, inspecting the occupants.

One of the horsemen, who wore a red sash, rode to my bed and lowered the right-side metal guardrail in the light of his torch. He activated a device that automatically raised me up. Then he drew a jeweled sword from his scabbard and was moving toward me, wielding it, as I let out a silent bellow and jumped out of the bed and into the chaise on my balcony.

My mind clear, I still kept seeing Emma's horrified reaction to one of my outbursts, or worse, her sympathetic one, imagined Emma offering to chain herself to me as Violet had done, and as much as it grieved me, I knew I had made the right choice in declining to see her again.

Part Two

CHAPTER FOURTEEN

Feeling stir-crazy, I had risked an outing to the Music Box Theatre and was settling into my seat (right-side orchestra to favor my good eye) after the intermission when the silenced phone in my pocket began buzzing incessantly. There were several missed calls and a message from Charlie: "I'm at Sardi's second-floor bar. Important you come immediately."

Sardi's, the legendary theater restaurant, was just down the street from the Music Box. I found Charlie sitting at the bar with a robust man he introduced with "John Williamson, meet Chet Tremaine.

"Sorry to pull you away," Charlie added while I ordered a drink. "It's not a very good show, anyway, and I knew you would want to hear what Mr. Williamson—"

"John," Williamson said.

"What John has to say . . . He came from San Francisco to close a deal of mine this afternoon, and he leaves on the redeye tonight. While we were having dinner he mentioned he'd only been in New York once before for his cousin's wedding, and that this cousin had an incurable disease that he miraculously cured by going to Nepal."

"It was called Bonnet syndrome," Williamson said, and I nearly upended the drink I was being handed. "Wasn't a doctor here in New York could do anything for him, but Bruce was a bit of a kook and he believed all kinds of spiritual stuff, so he knew about the gods and spirits and temples and healers and monks in Kathmandu. He and his family had been going through hell for many years, but after his visit to Kathmandu, he was completely cured. Never had another one of those crazy hallucinations."

"How about that, Chet?" Charlie said. "John is leaving tonight but I thought you ought to hear about this."

Part of me wanted to start laughing, under the assumption that Charlie would immediately join in in appreciation of his terrific joke: *Cured? Nepal?* Was the spiritual healer in Midtown all booked up? But there was no trace of humor in my friend's face. And after a moment I felt like I saw another face superimposed over his: smiling, hopeful. *Call. When you can.* It wasn't a hallucination. Just a feeling.

"You're damned right," I said. "Can you put me in touch with your cousin?"

"'Fraid not," Williamson said. "He got struck by lightning on a New Jersey golf course last year. But I could put you in touch with Sophie, his widow. She knows the whole shebang. Let's exchange cards."

He wiggled his wallet out of his butt pocket. I don't carry cards, so I wrote my vitals on the back of a Sardi's bar menu.

"I better get my ass out to the airport," Williamson said, consulting his wristwatch. "I'll call Sophie to tell her about you. I hope this does you some good."

I thanked him profusely as Charlie paid the bar bill. We

descended to the first-floor cloakroom, from where I grate-
fully carried his suitcase outside and we put him in a yellow
cab. Some of the shows were letting out and the sidewalk was
getting crowded. Charlie and I threw our arms around each
other and gave a couple of whoops.

There are a few good things that drizzle down on you from
above beyond your remotest expectations, and I thought this
was as good a one as I would receive this time around.

Sophie Gleason was immediately forthcoming and invited me
to her place in the Bronx. She wanted to hear about my encounters with the syndrome, as if authenticating my status.
I told her about the trapeze plus the wild ride on the MRI.

"Jehoshaphat, even worse than Bruce. Well, you certainly
need to escape your horrible Bonnet curse and I am only too
glad to help you best I can."

She was a voluble woman with a ripe Bronx accent somewhat softened by a few years at Rutgers.

"Do you mind if I ask you some personal questions?"

"Not at all. Ask away."

"Good. Are you religious?" she asked.

"Well, I don't belong to any organized religion but I believe
in God and the soul, so I guess you'd say that's my religion."

"All right . . . Bruce and I are Catholics, I mean were
Catholics, and when his syndromes were bad—that's what
we took to calling the hallucinations, his syndromes—he'd
go to church and pray to the statues of Mary and Jesus to
rescue him. But the syndromes didn't improve and he began
to seriously talk about suicide. At this point, to distract him,
a friend of his got him into his Nepali study group. Since
no one knows what causes the syndrome hallucinations and

Catholic prayers weren't being answered, we figured a civilization as old as Nepal's might have some impact for Bruce, maybe locating the basis of his hallucinations, something all our doctors had not been able to find. Oh yes, the brain is the source, they suggest, but where in the brain, they cannot say, although probing operations have been performed unsuccessfully. You follow me so far?"

"Yes, indeed."

Sophie continued. "Every aspect of life in Nepal is governed by hundreds of gods who have actual forms and are prayed to and regularly courted with offerings of flowers and food and other such daily gifts called *puja* that demonstrate the love the people have for the gods who dwell all over Kathmandu and spread their spirits in temples, trees, rivers, houses, schools, hospitals, restaurants. The two main religions are Hinduism and Buddhism, but there's a fair bit of intermixing. The Shiva *linga* and Buddhist *chaitya* even stand together in some places, and Hindus and Buddhists worship similar powers, although the names are different. With such a large number of creeds Bruce and I couldn't keep them straight—at the big festivals, of which there are a great many, everyone worships the most consulted deities: Ganesh, who with his distinctive elephant's head brings good luck, and Shiva, who responds to daily problems, often medical. Do you think you could make all this your mindset before going to Nepal? If you can't then it is a waste of time because you won't be able to connect. That's the thing about Bruce—he believed all this."

For even a chance to rid myself of the syndrome that had invaded and altered every aspect of my life? "I think I can, although it sounds like a lot of acceptance on my part."

"I've got all of Bruce's books for you, and all his notes—he kept a journal the entire time he was there."

"That's really kind of you. I'll be very careful with them. Does this Nepali group still exist?"

"No, 'fraid not. But I'll be happy to answer any questions you have once you get started."

"Is there someone there who . . ."

"Oh, yes, of course. I'll make up a list of persons, places, hotels, all that. But the fellow you want to start with is Dr. Shankar Gopal. He's not an MD, the 'doctor' is something else. He's a wonderful man who helped us every step of the way, an outstanding scientific palmist. Kathmandu is famous for its fortune-tellers, but Gopal, who used to read the king's palm every morning for His Highness to use as that day's guidance, is very scientific. Graduated Oxford, has a fabulous place on Durbar Square in Kathmandu. Outside the entrance is a famous fifteenth-century stone sculpture of Shiva with his beautiful wife, Parvati, sitting on his knee. Gopal will take care of everything for you, beginning with someone meeting you at the airport to take you to the Hotel Yak and Yeti."

I couldn't stop myself from laughing at the name. "Are there yaks wandering around the lobby?"

Sophie laughed too, though she shook her head. "It's five star and as impeccable as you could ask for. Well, what do you say? Does all my describing scare you off? There's even more stuff you ought to read up on before you go. I haven't even mentioned the *jhankri* you'll have to find with Gopal's help."

"What's that?"

"Who. A faith healer who intercedes between the person in need and the spirit world. In other words, he was the one who went into a trance and bridged Bruce into the invisible world of spirits. You'll have to accept him and his trances if you are going to make a go of finding your cure in Nepal."

"To answer your question, you certainly don't scare me off. Just the opposite. But does this call for a rather lengthy stay in Nepal? I run a business . . ."

"Oh, no, not long at all. Dr. Gopal will have everything prearranged for you. Either you connect or you don't. I'd say with Bruce it took maybe only a week or so to get under way."

"Did Bruce have some kind of psychic signal?"

"I don't quite remember, but when it happened and Bruce knew he was free of the Bonnet, that occurred on the day of the festival for Ganesh, a very important festival celebrated by Hindus and Buddhists. So we also got to celebrate Bruce's getting out from under the syndrome."

After going through all the items Sophie gave me, I realized that what it came down to was this simple proposition: to go through this ordeal on the other side of the globe, I would have to truly believe that a Hindu god could prevail over the Bonnet curse; that a *jhankri* medicine man in a trance could conjure up forces that would protect me; that monks and priests would imbue me with an emotional acceptance of the entire process.

As preposterous as it sounded, there was the indisputable fact that this very process had had "positive results" for Bruce, who, like me, had been suffering from the daily hideous assaults on his life.

Sitting on the terrace of my Connecticut cottage surrounded by the menacing syndrome structure blocking my view, I had a sharp yearning to discuss this dilemma with my father. He had meant so much in my life, but alas, he was no longer here. It was a sudden tragic accident, a second of time that decimated both Charlie and me.

Our fathers were as close friends as we are. All four of us would go to Yankees games together, to concerts; we'd fish out on the sound in Charlie's father's boat, a Chris-Craft. Once in a while our mothers would come along but only for the sea air, not to hook live bait on a fishing pole.

As we got older, Charlie and I fished less and less, but our fathers maintained their outings as often as their schedules would permit. Charlie's father was a distinguished surgeon at the Hospital for Special Surgery, my dad an architect with a prestigious firm in which he was a partner. No two families could have been any closer, but that dreadful accident changed all our lives.

It was a lovely sunny day when our fathers decided to run the Chris-Craft across the sound to Long Island, something they had done often in the past: eat lunch and fish over there. They were halfway across when a large ferry coming in the opposite direction rammed into them and split their boat in two, killing them both.

All these years later I still haven't been able to reconcile the loss of my closest, most indispensable friend. Nor has Charlie been able to handle the loss of his father. Neither of us has brothers or sisters. Charlie's mom moved to California after Charlie got married, and my mom married an Australian rancher she met in New York and now lives in Melbourne. All this has made Charlie and me like family, like two surviving brothers.

Charlie was of course interested in what came of the meeting with John Williamson at Sardi's bar. He was fascinated with my account of my talk with Sophie, and he looked at all the material she had given me. "It's a tough call," he said while we were having lunch at Rive Bistro. "I know the hell you are going through better than anyone, but going all the way to Nepal, where you have to deal with a palmist and a faith healer—that's one hell of a load, isn't it? Does any of that feel like something you can honestly open yourself up to?"

"Good God, Charlie, I don't know. It all seems forbidding, like sci-fi. But there's proof here it worked for Bruce, and if I don't give it a try and these wild attacks go on and on and on and get me down, I may have some punishing regrets." It had been weeks now since I'd seen her, but my thoughts still flashed to Emma. "And that's been our battle cry, hasn't it? No regrets!"

"You remember when we first came up with that? Back when we were just beginning to ski and those feisty hotshot teenagers challenged us to a race down the expert run . . ."

"And we beat them. Well, what would you do now?"

"I just couldn't deal with all that spiritual stuff. I'm too flat-footed. Have you discussed this with your Dr. Brevoro?"

"No. I know what he'd say."

"Don't be so sure. Some doctors have mystic streaks in them."

Dr. Brevoro took his time and went through all my Sophie stuff. "As a scientific, practical man who deals with medical problems, I have to say none of this seems possible. I accept that the state of a person's mind can have an influence on his physical body, but as far as I can tell, all these mystical attempts with vapors and bloodletting and idols don't seem to have the ability to achieve the desired effect."

"But they did on Bruce Gleason, and it may have the same effect on me, right?"

"I would have had to examine Mr. Gleason to comment on that. Mr. Tremaine, I know how badly Bonnet is impinging on your life, how desperate you are to be cured, but in my opinion going through this strange, bewildering ritual in Nepal, investing so much of yourself, your time, your money, and not achieving a resolution may make your disposition more depressed."

"Not my sunny disposition!" I laughed at that.

"I have one more thing for you to think about. In some patients Bonnet syndrome stops for a period of time, from weeks to years, and in some lucky ones, forever. No one can know what brings this about or when. Although you can't count on it, neither should you give up hoping."

That night, having a drink on my little New York balcony, I decided I had to make my mind up right then and there. I looked up to the heavens. A canopy of white bulbous clouds was overhead; three pigeons were strutting around, attracted by the seed I had scattered; Stravinsky was floating up from the balcony below. I felt at peace with the world when suddenly the pigeons erupted in squawking cries and turned into three black rats chasing each other. The frenzied alarm sounded by the disappeared pigeons and the syndrome substitution of the large, aggressive red-eyed rats running over my feet made my decision for me: I had to go to Nepal and take my chances or give up on any chance of peace or joy—or love—in my life again.

CHAPTER FIFTEEN

A driver with a Yak and Yeti placard with my name on it greeted me at the Kathmandu airport, and as Sophie Gleason had promised, yaks were not foraging in the lobby of the hotel. In fact, the hotel was luxurious, situated in a historic palace with a casino, landscaped gardens, tennis courts, antique fountains, a sauna, a business center, an outdoor swimming pool, and an impressive restaurant with an extensive Continental menu that served dishes that rivaled the five-star places of New York.

What Sophie had not described was the thick soup of carbon monoxide fog that had its poisonous arms wrapped around the city. Automobiles, trucks, buses, motorcycles packed the roads fender to fender. A suffocating heat added to the punishment. My morale suffered a wallop.

However, it recovered somewhat the next day when I took a taxi to Durbar Square, where Dr. Gopal's place was located. I was stunned by the sight of the square itself, a panorama of dozens of beautifully carved towers and twenty or thirty fascinating temples, the towers and temples each devoted to a particular god. I asked the driver to slowly drive me around and he described in his Nepali-accented English their origins, the powers of the different idols, and how their sites of worship were all still actively attended. It was a cavalcade of Nepali devotion, and at that moment I had a glimpse of hope that some of the god powers that had sustained the worshippers at these beautiful temples for so many centuries could pass on their positive influence to eradicate Bonnet's negative syndrome from my mind.

So it was with that more upbeat attitude that I rang the bell to Dr. Gopal's. The entrance was guarded by a huge stone statue of a god whom my driver identified as one of the most powerful: Shiva, seated, as Sophie had told me, with his wife in his lap.

Dr. Gopal was a tall, handsome man with a nicely trimmed beard and a perfectly fitted three-piece suit obviously of London origin, as was his impeccable English. His immense studio was furnished with graphic devices and models used in his palm-reading profession. A giant hand with its hills, valleys, and creases demarcated with symbols covered an entire wall. There were several small idols in lighted alcoves.

"So, Mr. Tremaine," he said as he poured two glasses of fruit juice from a crystal decanter, "you are here to follow in Mr. Gleason's footsteps. By the way, how is he? Still free of the Bonnet syndrome?"

I told him about the lightning strike.

"Ah, pity. He had me perform an in-depth palm analysis just before he left and I found a very ominous breach in his life line that I warned him about. But he was free of the syndrome before the lightning?"

"So I was told by his wife."

"Well, I hope you do as well with the Bonnet as he did. It

all depends on whether you can truly involve yourself with the gods and spirits. Only then can they produce a force that may eliminate the onslaught that has taken hold of you."

"Our doctors believe it comes from the brain."

"But they have not found where in the brain, have they?"

"No, that's why I am here. Not to face an incurable future."

"And we will do all we can to liberate you. Now, I will be in charge of your overall participation, all payments will be made to me, and I'll take care of everyone involved. But your primary contact has to be a *jhankri* and I have enlisted for you one of the most successful, Hari Karki, to work on your behalf."

"What does he do?"

"A *jhankri* deals with all the negative spirits that can torment people, unless they are placated. Like spirits of dead ancestors often attack descendants unless dissuaded by a *jhankri*, who is the only one who is able to establish contact with the spirit world, by going into a special trance. Nepali people believe in ghosts and witches whose spirits can cast spells, and the *jhankri* intercedes with them, arranging gifts like food, flowers, money, and such. Although known rather belittlingly as 'medicine men' and 'faith healers,' they are actually special people chosen at an early age for their ability to mediate between ordinary people and the spirit world, making their contact while in a special trance. The emergence of these people is rare and they are highly esteemed. Karki will be here shortly and you will see for yourself."

"Does that mean I have to make myself believe in ghosts and witches?"

"Not exactly. Karki will try to contact the evil spirits of your syndrome, if there are any. In his trance, the *jhankri* is able to deal with sickness, diagnostically and sometimes actually treating the illness and curing it. Think of him as a psychotherapist. His most powerful weapon, however, is his ability to align the evil spirits in his trance and arrange a solution to the spell they have cast, often offering his special gifts to the gods."

"But I have no gods . . ."

"You will. You have to open yourself up to all Karki prescribes if you are to be granted access to whatever spirits he finds who are torturing you."

The doorbell sounded. The thrum of drums filled the room. Dr. Gopal buzzed the door open. "That will be Karki," he said.

And in Karki came, an imposing man outfitted in his *jhankri* trappings. He was playing a double-headed decorated drum that was suspended around his neck. He wore a white pleated skirt and necklaces of *rudraksha* and various other seeds, mounted bells crisscrossed across his chest, and a headdress of braided multicolored cloth pieces. He was smiling and performing a little winding, hopping dance as he made his way to us.

"Hello, mister, how do you do," he said to me in accented English. He gave a quick bow of his head and grasped my hand in a solid two-pump shake. "I am honored," he said, "that we are to have a together."

Dr. Gopal poured Karki a glass of the fruit juice as he sat down beside me, pushing his drums out of the way. "Do you have open mind about need for special god for you and spirit that go here and there?"

"I'd believe in anything that would get rid of the syndrome that haunts me."

"Fine, good, very okay," Karki said.

He removed one of the straps from over his head and presented me with a sturdy traveling pouch. From it he withdrew a glaring statue, over a foot tall and obviously weighty. He held it out to me.

"So you will have the god Bhairav to take care of you when I chant. He is fierce, very fierce, with fangs and terrible eyes, but good for you since he is very very destroyer of evil. His seeing-everywhere eyes are all over—sides of buses, auto bumpers, carriages, golf carts, all over. You keep him in your room and give him nice things. We will take him with us to the evening prayers of the monks so he sees you do the monks' chants and maybe he sees you put your body in monks' holy stream. In the Yak and Yeti, every time you pass the Ganesh idol in the lobby you should put some coins in his basket. But you got to give much more gifts to a vicious god like Bhairav, who is not satisfied with flowers and milk but demands blood and alcohol."

I held him awkwardly. "I feed him my blood?"

"No, not yours," Dr. Gopal said. "But you will be part of a blood ceremony, the blood coming from one of these."

He handed me a list:

One.   Water buffalo . . . . . 750 dollars.

Two.   Black goat . . . . 450 dollars.

Three.   Sheep . . . . 300 dollars.

Four.   Duck . . . . 200 dollars.

Five.   Rooster . . . . 100 dollars.

"As you can see, the water buffalo is the most expensive and may even cost more than that, but his blood is powerful and most effective with a powerful idol like Bhairav. It is against the law to use a female."

"Is the buffalo killed in the ceremony?" I asked.

"Yes. There will be a ceremony, and special butchers who are in charge of the event."

"And I will be there?"

"Oh, yes, you and Bhairav will be part of it, along with monks and priests . . ."

"And especially me," Karki interjected. "I will try to make contact with Bhairav hoping that the buffalo's blood has happied him."

"Immediately after the blood ceremony, the butcher and his helpers will cut up the buffalo. The head is the butcher's fee, the carcass is yours."

"I'd like Karki to have it."

"Oh, thank you very kindly. The meat will be very special for my family."

"And perhaps you'd like to have the horns," Dr. Gopal said to me.

"No, I want to give them to you."

He accepted them enthusiastically.

"Well then, okay, all right," Karki said, "I will take you to the monks today and you will be with them for evening prayers. But not to dine. Monks eat not too tasty. You better off fancy stuff at Yak and Yeti."

I returned to the hotel, now for the first time fully aware of what I had gotten myself into. I found a table in one of the smaller gardens and ordered a glass of Sancerre from the wine list. As the red-jacketed waiter poured the Sancerre, I had a momentary feeling that I was a captive caught in the midst of a syndrome attack fraught with the blood of a water buffalo, a powerful idol that had to be fed blood and alcohol, chanting monks, spirits, and trances. I took a gulp of my Sancerre, put my head back, and looking at the streaky blue Kathmandu sky, I realized that this was not a hallucination but the real thing and either I could go on with this experience I'd brought upon myself or pack my bags, return to the States, and surrender to whatever the Bonnet syndrome had in store for me. I knew well that it was a grim future.

To be honest with myself, I had lived a life of compromise. A prime example: my relationship with Violet and her inexcusable father. I had paid a dear price for my ambivalence—the disastrous loss of my right eye. Would giving up on this attempt be another of my regrets? If I didn't see it through, I would always wonder. But then, could I really blend myself into the program lined up for me? Bruce Gleason had done just that, hadn't he? I had to admit I was somewhat intrigued by what I'd have to endure. My practical self knew it was an insane undertaking, but what was the alternative?

The red-jacketed waiter handed me a luncheon menu. Here was another choice: either order lunch and some more wine, or go to the concierge desk and book a return flight to New York.

"Would you like to order, sir," the waiter inquired, "or would you like a bit more time?"

I gave him a serious look, inhaled a long breath, and ordered the lamb and another glass of Sancerre.

CHAPTER SIXTEEN

Karki came to fetch me at the hotel in the morning.

"You have fed them?" he asked, gesturing to Bhairav's traveling pouch, which I had slung ungracefully over one shoulder.

"Just a touch of wine on my fingertip on his feet. But I don't have any blood . . ."

"Is okay. Not to worry. There is one drop of blood in each these little wrappers. Many people need blood for idols. Now we go to the monks. They know you come. I have talk to top monk. He talk English for you but not so good as me."

Carrying Bhairav in his traveling pouch, I followed Karki to the monks' retreat, which was in a verdant section of Kathmandu. Here the air was clean, and flowering bushes; tall, leafy trees; and a well-tended prolific vegetable garden surrounded the monks' edifice, a simple carved temple with a pair of life-size statues at the door. A thin stream of clear water ran along the rear of the temple.

The monks were doing yoga when we arrived. The head

monk disengaged himself and came to meet us. Karki introduced me: "This is supreme monk, Aga Kashyap."

"Most honored," Kashyap said as he bowed his shaved head. "We are most honored to receive you."

"I am very indebted," I replied.

"We help you to prepare yourself for when Karki seeks your negative spirits. So we welcome you to our yoga, to our meditation, our chant of om. So you know what om is we have this in English. Please to read, then you join us when yoga done. Maybe you take off shoes, sit on bench, put feet in stream. Meditate till we start om."

He handed me a paper with a description of om in English.

I removed my shoes, sat down on the stone bench, and gingerly put my feet into the stream. I closed my eyes and meditated. I had belonged to a yoga group when I was in college, and we did a bit of chanting and meditating back then, but this was different, more profound.

The monks rose in unison, chanting a very resonating om. I walked across the stream and joined them with my eyes closed, head laid back, feeling a communion with the clustered oms, deep and varying in intensity.

Before leaving, Aga Kashyap invited Karki and me for tea. He also invited me to come for the next two days of om and meditation, with the third day scheduled for Karki's ceremony. He said a group of monks would be there as well as some priests, and they would "pray that Karki will make contact with what he seeks" for me.

That evening I had dinner at the Y and Y, and the syndrome let me know it was still on the scene by sprinkling miniature clusters of its signature pine needles on my dishes.

The next two days passed quickly. Lois sent several important publishing queries I had to attend to, I kept my rendezvous with the monks, I fed money to the Ganesh in the lobby, I visited a few of the more spectacular temples with Karki as my guide, and I fed Bhairav his ration of wine and blood and talked to him, urging him to help Karki; as long as I had put myself in this position, I thought, I may as well go all the way.

Dr. Gopal phoned me and said that Karki's trance had been arranged for four o'clock that afternoon and I should come to his place a half hour before and he would accompany me there. "Do not forget to bring Bhairav."

I took a taxi to beautiful Durbar Square with Bhairav in tow and got off at Dr. Gopal's decorated door. All day following his call, I had been building a growing apprehension about the impending event. My mind was a jumble. I had been in Durbar Square many times over the past days, visiting the temples and towers, and I had seen many events honoring idols—marriages, birthday celebrations, and the like—and I was now much more familiar with Nepali customs.

"May I look at your hand before we leave?" Dr. Gopal asked.

"Of course."

He pressed my right hand against an inking pad that made all the hills and valleys of my hand stand out in bold relief. Using several instruments, powerful magnifiers, and electrodes that tickled my palm, he studied the area intently, wrote symbols and numbers on a sheet filled with strange diagrams and hieroglyphs. He placed all his papers in a file that he put in a desk drawer.

"What did you see?" I asked.

"This is just raw data. Now I must evaluate everything. Shall we go?"

"Should we call a taxi?"

"Not necessary. It's at the ceremonial palace just beyond the bend over there. An easy walk."

Oh, no, for God's sake, I thought as a panicky chill attacked me. *I'll be a public spectacle.* I had taken it for granted that Karki would perform his trance privately. But no, this was going to be a touristy show with this pathetic creature from New York on view.

As we rounded the bend a burgeoning display confronted us. Camera-bearing tourists were already beginning to cluster. The domed stone ceremonial edifice had steps like shelves, on which Karki was placing large decorated idols. We walked over to him and I handed him Bhairav from his carrying bag.

"Ah, mister, hello, good day. These are my own idols: Surya, sun; Agni, fire; Indra, rain. I bring them to join Bhairav when I do my trance in the rain of blood." He indicated a tall standing sheet of thick clear plastic adjacent to the ledge on which the idols were arranged.

"You should stand behind here when rain of blood comes."

I noticed he was wearing a special gold embossed tunic that I presumed was indicative of his impending trance.

A little conclave of musicians now started to play. "They are here to help when I go to trance to find Bonnet syndrome spirits," Karki said.

The music was quite good—cymbals, hand drums, conch-shell horns, and bells strapped across the torsos and to the ankles of the musicians—but I was in no mood to enjoy it. A group of nine monks had assembled, along with a phalanx of priests. A stream of camera-bearing tourists was invading the area, snapping their hungry cameras at everything. I pulled the brim of my cap down to conceal my face as much as I could. The camera crowd now reluctantly parted for the white-clad butcher and his two assistants, who were leading an enormous water buffalo to an embedded post that was immediately in front of the four idols—and me. The butcher had an embossed silver-handled knife tucked in a scabbard in his waistband. The buffalo was at least seven feet in height across his flanks, and his two heavy horns jutted from the sides of his head. He was tied securely to the post. The music intensified. The butcher's assistants began to pour buckets of water on the head of the buffalo, who stomped and protested. The tourists jockeyed each other for camera positions.

"The ritual butchers pour the water," Dr. Gopal explained to me, "to make the buffalo shake his head up and down: that is regarded as permission for the butcher to proceed." The priests put a flame to a tall stack of pungent incense.

The buffalo finally gave his horned head a monstrous shaking, spraying water all around, and the solemn butcher drew his silver knife from its scabbard and made his way to the buffalo. Karki started to perform a complicated, twirling, hopping dance, sounding his drums and emitting strange vocalizations. I presumed he was entering his trance.

I was mesmerized, in fact paralyzed, by what was unfolding and felt powerless to interfere. I called out to Dr. Gopal but the noise of the tourists, the music, Karki's intonations, the protesting buffalo, and the monks and priests with their lamentations completely drowned out my attempt to reach him. It was not unlike being blanketed under the influence of the Bonnet.

While his assistants each held fast to a horn, the butcher plunged his knife into the side of the buffalo's powerful neck, severing his jugular vein, blood spurting forward in a dense stream, like water going full blast from a garden hose. The butcher directed the streaming blood in the direction of the idols, where it bathed them in red, the spray also striking the plastic shield protecting me. I recoiled in shock and pulled my cap down over my eyes, steadying myself by pressing against the shield. There was a crescendo of tumultuous noise as the buffalo began to stagger. Karki had now assumed a set position, the drums cast aside as he uttered a flow of words I didn't know.

My eyes were mesmerized into watching the tragedy of the beleaguered buffalo, who, as the flow of blood waned, stumbled, and with a final surrendering cry catapulted onto his side, dying. The butchers immediately sprang into action, getting their paraphernalia from their cart and starting to dismember the buffalo, the chief butcher sawing off the horned head while the others began to carve up the rest of the body and fill their cart with the pieces.

My tolerance was at a breaking point; this animal's death was all my doing. A self-anger was rising in me. Too cowardly to face up to the strident threats to my life, I had sought this impossible escape without caring about its consequences. I had to get myself out of here. My sense of guilt was fueling my anger.

There was a beautifully carved temple in back of us: I slipped away from my blood-splattered shield and stole out the rear of this ceremonial structure and into the temple. It was completely deserted. Clusters of tall candles were burning. There were scores of idols in their niches scattered all over the temple. I had undertaken something without fully understanding it; I was still as much of a fraud as I had been as Lance Dixon's prospective son-in-law. I sat down on a stone-carved bench feeling empty and deserted and compromised.

CHAPTER SEVENTEEN

The following morning I went to Dr. Gopal's studio to settle my account. My return flight for New York was scheduled for the next day.

"That was one of the finest trance ceremonies I have ever witnessed," Dr. Gopal said. "Karki was in great form. He will be here shortly."

I told him how upsetting the sacrifice of the buffalo was for me.

"I can understand, but the gods demand sacrifice if we are to communicate successfully." He picked up the sheet of paper that was spread in front of him. "I have not yet completed my analysis of your hand. You have a strange constellation I have not seen before."

"Favorable or unfavorable?"

"That's what I have to determine. Where it is leading you. It is a crossroad on top of a crossroad. There are some complicated things I must perform to make that determination. I will be sending you my findings."

He was handing me my accounting as the doorbell jingled,

and with the sound of Karki's drums preceding him, in he came. He bowed and shook hands with each of us, then took off his drums and laid them beside his chair.

"Now, mister, that was a very, very good ceremony, wasn't it, Dr. Gopal?"

"Yes, my very words."

"I was impressed," I said, "but did you make contact with the Bonnet syndrome forces?"

"Ah, yes, your syndrome. I did make contact but with so many, many, many thousands of spirits out there, it is big problem to make sure I deal with single one I seek, you understand?"

"Well, yes, but what do you think? Will they lay off me?"

"Maybe yes, maybe no. I go now to my idols, wipe off blood, see what they say. You go back U.S. today?"

"No, tomorrow."

"I make Bhairav clean and bring to you at hotel to take to USA," he said as Dr. Gopal handed him an envelope that I presume was his part of my payment. "I polish up his fangs and give him nice new hair and make face more mean. He take good care of you, drive away evil."

"Thank you, Karki."

"I wish you very nice everything." He shook my hand, dipped his head, retrieved his drums, and made his way out the door.

Dr. Gopal sat back in his chair, touched the tips of his fingers across his chest, and gave me a thoughtful look.

"You are disappointed, yes? I see the look on your face, which is like the one I saw on the faces of my fellow Oxford students when we used to discuss the things Nepalis believe in, how important *jhankri* like Karki are for many who endure torment and painful suffering. It is a known fact that much painful suffering is mental, and the *jhankri* are really their psychotherapists, who through trances and the complicated use of idols are able to eradicate the illusion of pain and fear of imagined illness. So it is with *jhankri* like Karki who prepare their own medicines made from herbs and plants, perform physical treatments, exorcisms, relay positive messages they induce from outlying spirits."

"Like he tried for me, but it's not a sure thing, is it?"

"No, but who else is there to intercede between the petitioners who say their prayers, full of need and sorrow and pain, and those who can answer those prayers? Just consider how many prayers fill the world every day. Christian prayers in churches, children at their bedsides, Muslims with their foreheads on mats, Jews lighting their candles, Catholics from their kneeling entreaties, on and on, thousands upon thousands filling the heavens with their invocations and appeals. Who's to sort any one from any other? Here in Nepal, *jhankri* perform that very difficult function, and if they find they have to sacrifice a buffalo to do that, then that is how it must be. I hope Karki will help you. You are suffering and it is important to hope that things will improve for you. That Karki will be able to chase your bedevilers."

He poured two drinks from a crystal bottle.

"May your cloud be lifted and the sun prevail."

We drank.

"There is one last thing I wish to do for you, Mr. Tremaine. It is something I have not been able to perform for anyone else, but I am very impressed with your need. There is a Nepali woman who receives very few people, especially foreigners, but she has consented to see you today if you are willing."

"A woman?"

"In fact, a self-declared goddess."

"You mean another carved figure like Bhairav?"

"No, a real-life figure. Let me explain: The power to de-
stroy evil is wielded by the goddess Durga, who has been
worshipped for centuries. She is the goddess of war, the
protector against demonic forces. To remind people of the
presence of Durga, a council of high priests selects young
girls who measure up to certain qualifications, such as 'legs
like a deer, chest like a lion, neck like a conch shell, eyelashes
like a cow,' and so forth. They finally choose one girl whom
they put in an isolated room that is scattered with the sev-
ered heads of water buffaloes that are dripping blood, like
the one at your ceremony. If the girl survives this ordeal she
is considered ready to become Kathmandu's Royal Kumari.
In a second procedure at the Taleju Temple, the spirit of the
Durga goddess takes hold of her body. While a goddess, she
is established in the beautiful Kumari Ghar with people who
treat her royally, and she presides over a shrine in her honor.
She comes to an end of her being a Royal Kumari before she
has her period and sheds menstrual blood. That brings me
to this woman. Her name is Kishani. When her menstrua-
tion ended her life as a Kumari goddess and the high priests
found a successor, Kishani refused to return to being a girl
and proclaimed herself a continuing goddess. She went to live
in a secluded temple in the forest, where she only sees those
who have status and come with gifts to pay her homage. It is
considered a great feat to get her blessing. She has consented
to see you, if you so desire. What do you say?"

We trekked through the forest in the late afternoon and Gopal
led us expertly to her half-hidden temple, small in scale with

two steeples. It was on an abrupt rise with carved stone fig-
ures lining the path up to the temple's entrance, a golden bell
with a knocker hanging beside the carved door. Dr. Gopal
struck the bell three times, and a servant opened the door
and led us inside to a terrace on the opposite side, where a
woman in a long, stark black dress sat on a high thronelike
chair reading.

Upon seeing us she rose and greeted Dr. Gopal. She was
quite beautiful. Her indigo hair set off the ivory color of her
skin. She was tall and very thin, with striking necklaces of
various seeds and gems wound around her neck. In perfect
English she asked if our trek had been pleasant.

"Very," I said. I complimented her on her English.

"Dr. Gopal arranged lessons for me all through my Royal
Kumari goddess years at the Kumari Ghar."

Gopal introduced me. She studied me with her penetrating painted eyes set deep in her ivory face, a third eye painted
on her forehead.

"You are beset by a syndrome that attacks you?"

"Yes, it has a severe hold on me, ever since my eye—"

"I know. Dr. Gopal has told me all about you."

"I am most grateful," I said.

Dr. Gopal said, "Mr. Tremaine has sent a generous contri-
bution that I will leave with your attendant. Now I must go
back to serve my clients."

"Thank you, Dr. Gopal. I will return Mr. Tremaine in my
carriage with my attendant."

They shook hands, he left, and she returned her attention
to me. She picked up a small fipple flute with her left hand
and a tabor drum with her right. "I will send a message about
you to goddess Durga, who is my mentor."

She sat down and started to play the fipple flute with her

left hand while sustaining the rhythm with her right. She often interrupted the flute to sing snatches of a song in Nepali, which, I suppose, was directed to Durga.

"Look to the sky, Mr. Tremaine," Kishani said, "and find your star, your personal star, the one that stands out, that captures your eye. Bathe in the light of that star and kiss the gentle wind caressing your face. From now on you must follow that star, wherever it goes. You will remember this song and you let it lead your way."

She played the song with feeling, her eyes closed, her body swaying, and I closed mine and felt a rapture I had never felt before.

"Now, we will enter my personal chamber and try to make contact."

She led me over to a magnificently carved cabinet with a mother-of-pearl interior and gold strands crisscrossing the ceiling. There was just enough room for the two of us. She took one of the jeweled necklaces from around her neck, garnets I think, and put it around mine. She lit a small stick of floral incense and poured two crystal glasses of red wine. "Enter into my spiritual vein, Chet Tremaine, pledging yourself with this commitment." We touched glasses and drank to each other. "When I was a Kumari goddess, this likeness was made of me." She took a small statue from an overhead shelf and handed it to me. It did resemble her. She also handed me a CD that contained her love song to the star. "Whenever you have to overcome some problem, let me sing to you on this disc in front of my likeness. I will hear you and help you with your problem, even pass it along to goddess Durga."

She sat me down and tattooed a little turtle on one of my feet. "He is my symbol," she said. She repeated the turtle at the base of my thumb. "Please do not leave me. I have many followers. I will pray for you at night, under the stars, with spirits I know."

She put her goddess likeness and my CD in a traveling sack and escorted me out the door, where a small horse-drawn carriage was waiting. She put her arms around me and kissed me on my lips, holding the kiss as her attendant opened the carriage's door. She pulled back and smiled at me.

"This is Samandori. He knows the way through the forest and will take you to the Y and Y. I wish you great good happenings."

"And I return the wish to you," I said.

The carriage rumbled away. I stretched out in the backseat and tried to straighten out my whirling senses. I inspected the reality of the thumb turtle to try to authenticate my encounter with the goddess. It wasn't a genuine tattoo, only a transfer with a heavily gummed adhesive.

The following day, when I packed my bag, I put Bhairav and goddess Kishani side by side. To my eyes, they made a nice-looking couple.

Part Three

CHAPTER EIGHTEEN

M y journey back to the United States was an uplifting taste of freedom, a salute to Karki, a life without molestation. My last meal at the hotel had no sprinkling of fake green sprigs, the toilet in the airplane did not have a grid over the surface of the water as it had on my flight to Nepal, and by the time we touched down at Kennedy and a cab deposited me at my apartment, there was no sign of Bonnet's menace.

I tested my right eye to determine if perhaps my eyesight had miraculously returned, but it hadn't, so this respite had to be credited to the ministrations in Nepal. Quite possibly Karki had made some kind of contact, but that was hard for me to believe, although the great universal belief in redeeming spirits was something that had to be acknowledged.

Thanks to Lois, my office had functioned very well in my absence, although there were a few prickly items that needed my attention—not to mention the looming specter of the Tee case, though the trial was still a couple months out. So I dealt first with the most crucial matter at hand: a letter from an illustrious publisher interested in speaking to me about representing his firm on retainer. With my head clear of the syndrome's interference, I was inclined to take on this prestigious new client. I sent him a letter to that effect and invited him to lunch.

I went out to my place in Connecticut for the weekend and was elated to find no trace of the dread syndrome. The despicable high blocking fence was gone, and once more I had my open vista of sky and uninterrupted greenery. The floor of the bathroom was unmarked and the water in the toilet bowl was not covered.

That evening I had a lighthearted dinner at Pane e Bene with Charlie and Lydia, enjoying the jocularity of Alessandro, our philosophical waiter. We toasted my liberation from Bonnet syndrome with a good bottle of Valpolicella (Lydia refrained maternally), and the road home was unmolested.

We had a nice chat on my moon-flooded terrace, and I went to bed with an abundance of benign feeling as a result of my reinstated enjoyment of my Connecticut retreat.

But in the dead of night a familiar jolt woke me from my sleep and deposited me in the cramped overhead section of a speeding passenger train. I was on my back, my face close to the pitching ceiling of pipes and wires.

The seats below me were filled with passengers whom I immediately recognized as the people I had encountered in that dreadful syndrome episode where I was on the sidewalk on my back and no one would give me a hand to help me up. I now yelled over the train's noise to get someone's attention, but as before no one looked up, not even the conductor, who was collecting tickets. I started to ease myself forward, pushing with my hands in back of me, hoping to find an exit from this imprisonment. But it was endless, a continuing push into an area of darkness—punishment, as I saw it, for my attempted Nepali foray into freedom.

I intensified my entreaties to those below, calling as loud as I could, pounding on the metal, but to no avail. I tried to turn over but there wasn't enough room to raise myself up. I had a small red Swiss Army knife in my pocket, but what good would it do me? There was nothing I could cut with it. My wrists, I thought, smiling at my own limp humor.

The train was beginning to slow down, and as I continued to edge forward, I was getting entangled with a section of complicated cables and hissing pipes and intertwined wires that were giving off sparks. There were blinking colored lights that I followed into a narrow chasm that imprisoned me above the exit ramp of the train, where all the passengers were deboarding. The area was crowded with porters; police; vendors of food, souvenirs, and periodicals; train personnel; men and women in uniform; passengers arriving and departing. I shouted at those who came near, but my voice was thoroughly well shot by now, and rapping on the glass with my knife was feeble and attracted no response. The whooshing volume of steam emanating from the hissing pipes was noticeably increasing, the heat and lack of visibility of my area beginning to affect me. I found it increasingly difficult to breathe and to see anything through the curtain of thick steam. I had to gasp for air and I pounded frantically on the glass with my folded knife, praying someone would respond. My good eye was now completely blinded by the steam. My mouth was a furnace trying to suck in resisting air. My breath became a cough, deeper and deeper as I fought to keep conscious, trying to draw a fragment of air into my lungs but losing the fight, until with a desperate piercing sound I threw myself forward and, coughing heavily, fell on the floor beside my bed, clutching the mangled bedclothes, my torn pillow over my face.

I pulled myself up and grabbed the bottle of water on my nightstand. I desperately uncapped it and gulped it dry. My mind was disoriented and I continued to inhale deep draws of air. I lowered myself onto the bed, shut my eyes, and tried to steady myself on the pitching sea. Waves crashed: the horrible ride on the imaginary train, the surrendering cry of the Nepali water buffalo, the mounting cases at my office, and the ever-present knowledge that I had Bonnet syndrome, I would forever have Bonnet syndrome. It was as if I had been conked on the head with a two-by-four wielded by Violet's father.

There was another bottle of water on the nightstand. I poured some on my face and on the top of my head, the water lifting me and becoming the windshield wiper of my frazzled mind. The fog slowly cleared away and took the illusion of freedom with it. The disillusion of the Bonnet had reasserted itself, and I would have to settle for being its hostage for the rest of my life.

I managed to wrap my terry-cloth robe around myself and pad out onto the terrace. There was moonlight, but the awful altitudinous fence was even more decrepit and even higher than I remembered it. It blocked my view of the delicate branches of the white birch, the glistening leaves of the chestnuts, and the unruly sassafras. I was still coughing and wheezing but I staggered across the grass to the reflecting pool to pay homage to the trio of giant koi who had been there as long as I had. I sat there on the stone bench, watching them perform their graceful dances with a retinue of lesser koi attending them. I was suddenly swept back to sitting on the stone-carved bench of the Nepali monks, with my feet in their crackling stream. A rush of sadness came over me. Sad that I had been so desperate for a miracle. Sad I had throttled what little hope I had to free myself from the unending humiliation of the Bonnet syndrome. Until now I had foolishly tried to combat this affliction, trying to deny Dr. Brevoro's reality. Well, no more. I knew I now had no choice but to surrender—not to despair, but to reality. I had to find a way to live with that reality and concentrate on what I had that was enjoyable and positive while soldiering up to the negative emanations as best I could.

One of the koi broke the surface and splashed back down, which caused me to recall that previously the pool's surface had invariably been covered by artificial syndrome garden waste, but perhaps this was a signal that the syndrome was going to be a bit more forgiving. It was a minor thing, this clear, exposed water, but it was something positive to cling to when I felt like I was drowning.

CHAPTER NINETEEN

My new resolve to accept Bonnet syndrome for what it was and stop trying to combat it was aided and abetted by the grace of being very busy and distracted, my mind focused on other things. The Tee trial still lurked, ominous, on my calendar, and I was yet to figure out if I was capable of winning it—or even conducting myself professionally for its duration. Meanwhile, the—mostly self-imposed—deadline for the next Jefferson Honeywell adventure was approaching as well. There, at least, I found myself blessed with a sudden breakthrough: what if the perpetually single detective finally found love? Words flew from my fingers once I began crafting the story of Honeywell's life-changing chance encounter with a beautiful jazz singer, whose career had been temporarily derailed by an accident that left her wheelchair-bound. The connection this unlikely pair formed reinvigorated them both.

It wasn't entirely without self-awareness that I composed these pages. Merely that, thus far, it was only within the confines of my fiction that I could express what was boiling inside me.

And so little by little, like a wandering creek finding its path, I settled into an existence that afforded me the best chance of enduring with Bonnet syndrome intrusions. Once again, I began avoiding social engagements, as it made me more and more uncomfortable having to deal with people and conditions that nobody else was aware of. I still saw Charlie and Lydia but not very often, even though they were most solicitous about my syndrome, always inquiring when I was with them about what was happening to me that they weren't able to discern. In New York I ate dinners alone at one or two comfortable places where I often brought a book to the table as my companion. Weekends in Connecticut I would mostly bring frozen gourmet meals obtainable from two outstanding places: Maria's Kitchen on Third Avenue and William Poll on Lexington. I would put a meal in the microwave, following directions, and dine on the terrace, good weather permitting, or in front of the television. At first, the invading syndrome characters were upsetting, but there were nights they didn't show up, and the nights they did I eventually taught myself how to concentrate on somehow disregarding them. Don't look at them, pretend they are not there, pretend you are like everyone who's not so afflicted, don't let your emotions get the better of you.

To my surprise, on late Connecticut nights when I felt an emptiness close to despair, I would go to Bhairav, who sat on a windowsill, his fierce scowl and beard dominating the living room, and feed him a daub of gin on his belly and a drop of blood on his foot. Karki had come to the Yak and Yeti just before I left, with a bundle of blood packs to take with me and advice: feed Bhairav regularly, tell him your troubles, explain that you need his help and his great powers, and if he likes you, he may be able to help you. What have you got to lose? On those melancholy nights I even lit lavender incense and played Nepali music.

Then in one week I received two interesting pieces of mail. The first was from my ex-fiancée, Violet Dixon: a gold-embossed announcement of her marriage to Dexter von Beideihof. I was glad that Violet had found someone, but I thought about calling Dexter and warning him to duck when Lance R. A. Dixon forces him to play tennis and goes up for a fatal overhead.

The second was a letter from Dr. Gopal telling me that he had completed his in-depth assessment of my hand with this conclusion: that I may have sidestepped some of my current troubles, but that there was a strong indication that some un-expected episode would occur that would in some way reset my existence—who I was and what I did.

CHAPTER TWENTY

I was enjoying one of my now-rarer lunches with Charlie when out of the blue, he asked about Emma Vicky—or, as he still called her, "sleeve lady." He did not reveal his source but he seemed to have recently come to know a considerable amount about Ménière's.

"One thing's for sure," he said, "she may have vertigo, twirl and tumble a lot now, but as time passes it may decrease."

"Charlie, I can't help but feel like you're leading the witness."

Charlie laughed. "No, no . . . I'm just saying, if she's as wonderful as I remember you saying she is, it would be a pity if she continues to shut herself away for all time. Maybe you should call her up. Perhaps Lydia and I can—?"

His phone rang and he quickly answered, spoke for a few seconds, and pushed up from the table. "It's Lydia. The baby's coming, she's heading to the hospital. Wish us good luck. I'll phone you." And he was hurriedly on his way. I was genuinely elated for him with just a touch of envy. Being a syndrome victim as I was, I couldn't see myself, given my limitations, being much of a father.

But Charlie, it seemed, already had some of my own father's magic: He'd laid it plainly in front of me, what I should do. What I *wanted* to do.

Despite the fact that I hadn't seen Emma in months, my mind had never left her. In our short time together, I had been physically drawn to her, but it was more than that—or it could have been. But I had convinced myself that burdening her with my neediness would double her load instead of considering the possibility that the two of us carrying on together might be able to halve it.

Knowing that across the city, Lydia was laboring to launch a whole new life into the world, I summoned my own courage and phoned Emma. I was braced for any number of reactions, from anger to indifference, but instead Emma expressed only delight to hear from me after so long. Her lovely, lyrical voice was everything I remembered.

A few minutes' discussion revealed that her birthday was approaching, and emboldened as I was, I suggested the time had come for her to overcome her fear of having a Ménière's attack in a restaurant and convinced her that together we could take chances. She was not quite sure but when I offered to make a reservation at Maialino, a fine restaurant that we could walk to on the other side of Gramercy Park, she decided, yes, it was time.

It proved to be a splendid foray. The moment we laid eyes on each other again, everything that had hung between us seemed to snap back into place within the space of a breath. We walked to the restaurant arm in arm, she looking even more beautiful in her birthday finery. We were seated in a small banquette facing each other. My only syndrome pestilence was a sprinkling of strange-shaped flora on top of the warm bread in its basket, unobserved, of course, by Emma, who remained sprightly and confident despite the threat of her Ménière's.

On the way back from the restaurant, Emma felt a little whirly from looking up at the half-moon overhead, so we sat down on a bench and talked for a while and I could feel a subtle change in how we were with each other.

After the success of her birthday dinner, I started seeing Emma more and more often—in a way it felt as if the entire time we'd been apart, we'd actually been together; I could feel the ghost of her presence in my memories of Nepal. Though we agreed to take things slow, physically, emotionally—well, it was the most sudden and most complete connection certainly that I'd ever felt with any woman, any other person. We enjoyed our time together, often reading Shakespearean plays in which she had performed, and I sometimes got her to sing Shakespearean sonnets with her guitar (sonnets that she had sung on the tour of her group). I brought dinners to her from places like Maria's Kitchen (chicken curry) and William Poll (cheese soufflé). Emma continued to overcome her Ménière's reticence and we were able to go to more restaurants and even the ballet, where a stage full of spinning dancers induced some trauma but she recovered before the final curtain fell. And if clowns or spots appeared, I found I was able to successfully ignore them. I focused instead on the warmth of Emma beside me, the weight of her hand in mine.

CHAPTER TWENTY-ONE

The day after our interrupted lunch and the crucial call that brought Emma back into my life, Charlie phoned me. In an elated voice, he related that the birth had been easy as easy could be and asked if I would like to come take a look at handsome Alfred Epps, who had a full shock of hair and a great pair of shoulders. Alfred, named after Charlie's father, was indeed a great-looking baby, and I was very happy for Charlie, standing there with my arm around my friend's shoulders as he exuded fatherly wonderment in this miracle that had happened to him and Lydia.

A few weeks later, once mother and baby were safely home and settled, I took Charlie to Tavern on the Green for a proper celebration. Sidestepping for now the fresh new thing with Emma, I used the occasion to air my concerns about the Tee case—the trial, as he well knew, was now mere weeks away. Since my poor showing in the deposition, I knew I would have to rely more than ever on Charlie to keep me in check.

"So, Charlie, since I can't seem to get out of trying this case, will you at least be my wingman?"

"Of course, Chet, but I'm worried, I'll be out of my league—I'm not a proper litigator. Are you sure you can't get someone like Lionel McCaffell?"

"Tried him. Not free . . ."

"Otto Freeley?"

"Out of the country."

"Well, I'll do all I can to find somebody to help us out. I'll call around. Must be somebody. What about your associate?"

"Lois is great but she has no trial experience. You've been in the trenches with me; I trust you."

Though he kept spouting caveats, Charlie, like I knew he would, agreed.

The next evening, when I was at dinner with Emma, she asked me why I looked so troubled. On this night we were having dinner in an Italian place near her apartment. I told her about my ongoing dilemma.

"The last cross-examination . . . I was awful, confused. I would never trust myself again because the syndrome will surely pull the same trick. Being in a courtroom, with a jury and members of the press in the gallery, is a recipe for disaster."

"You see? Giving in like that! That's what you and I talked about. Only makes it worse."

The waiter arrived with our bottle of Chianti and a platter of calamari.

"But if I fumble again on this one and lose, the verdict would be really costly and more humiliating. It's a tough case as it is."

"Not if you go in there believing in yourself. And really mad at these syndrome bastards. Let me tell you something: When I was cast in a West End play for the first time, I came onstage in that big theater and faced that sea of people, including the main critics, and I truly lost my way. Botched my lines. Fumbled my stage directions . . ."

"That was me stammering at my witness—botched everything."

"My first reaction was shame. I thought I should let my understudy replace me—in fact I was sure the director was going to do just that—but after a sleepless kind of night, I got up the next day feeling angry for knuckling under and disgracing myself onstage. I had lunch with my mother, who gave me a big hug of congratulations. 'What for?' I asked. 'I was pitiful.' My mother got a laugh out of that. 'You had a little first-time jitters, that's all. You were just fine.' I said, 'No, I wasn't. I expect to be replaced for tonight's performance.' 'Oh, darling,' she said, 'nonsense. All the good things in you will find your way for you.'

"As it turned out the director didn't replace me—only gave me a few notes—and I inhaled the applause that washed over me that following night."

Our second course arrived, veal Milanese on the bone topped with arugula, which we shared.

"In other words, you think I should stay on the case and make myself face a jury again—probably with a pack of syndrome interlopers in the jury box, unseen by the judge?"

She fixed her gold-flecked eyes on me. "Yes, yes," she said, "yes. And what's more, I'll give you an IOU to cover a negative verdict if there is one."

We both laughed at that.

"How about this—you told me the TV guy you're doing the voice-over for wants you to do a commercial for the same Brit sponsor but you turned him down."

"Yeah. I told him about my unpredictable Ménière's . . ."

"But you said he didn't care, that it's easy to start and stop shooting. Yet you still turned him down, right?"

"I did."

"All right. Tell you what—you do the commercial and I'll do the trial, even though the courtroom will probably be packed with syndrome fakes. We can each practice our lines in front of each other the night before. What do you say?"

She gave me a scrunched-up look. Drained her wine. Plunked down the glass emphatically. "I don't know if we are good or bad for each other," she said.

CHAPTER TWENTY-TWO

No matter how much time one has to prepare for trial, it's never enough. I had to read and analyze all the depositions plus all the discovery materials. I had to coach Penelope on how to answer questions truthfully and effectively like last time, except with the eyes of the jury on her. I took all of this to my apartment to avoid distraction. Of course there were plenty of the usual syndrome invaders—floating objects like blue scarves and dancing music notes, and the occasional appearance of a woman in a silk gown trimmed in fur and a man blowing a soundless bugle—but by now I had made myself somewhat immune to their effects, as if repetition were a vaccine.

I reread *Topiary* a few more times, re-studying the passages about Cespuglio and the poem. The more I read, the more I became aware of the somber challenge I faced.

I had taken to ferrying Bhairav and Kishani back and forth with me between the country and the city—they were very well-traveled idols—and more than once I took him off his shelf and told him my troubles. Better to talk to him than to myself. I had sustained the ritual of anointing him with daubs of wine and blood, indulging myself in believing, as the Nepali did, that he might bring me good luck. Whenever I doubted, I always countered it with the same refrain, my own little version of Pascal's wager: *Why not? What have I got to lose?*

Also, most nights, before going to sleep, I'd assume my yogic position on the floor, close my eyes, and chant a series of oms, putting my mind in a kind of neutral holding while I tried to eject any adverse emanations.

I interrupted my trial preparation for the baptism of Charlie and Lydia's son. Lydia wore a new flowery dress; Charlie, who was mostly indifferent to clothes, wore a new shirt, tie, and pocket square; and baby Alfred wore a handsome new baptism gown. I presented Alfred with a silver Tiffany rattle. He was the epitome of a picture-perfect baptism baby. Charlie was overloaded with fondness for him, as was Lydia. I could appreciate Charlie's feeling about the baby he had named in honor of the father who had been so cruelly wrenched from his life, as my co-adventurer, teacher, and advisor had been wrenched from mine. I was very thankful to be named Alfred's godfather.

When Lydia picked him up at the end of the ceremony, she asked if I would like to hold him. He looked at me as if I really interested him, and I looked at him with a fatherly surge of feeling. I had been concerned with my personal day-to-day problems, with no thought of a future that I could address with reasonable hope and desire. Now, with this newborn baby in my arms, listening to the little gurgling sounds coming from him, I envied Charlie's freedom to be able to create a new life. Bubbling inside me was a strange, impossible yearning to have a baby bearing my own father's name in my arms.

I accompanied Emma in a taxi to the M. G. Bates Studio for her commercial. She was trying to overcome her trepidation but I knew that for her it was somewhat like facing the gallows. She was adamant that I not go into the studio with her; she would call for me later when she was finished.

I was inordinately nervous for her, about not her performance but her ability to withstand the pressure without succumbing to Ménière's penalties.

She was waiting for me at the studio door when I got there, and as I entered she came to me with a smile as beatific as the rise of the sun on a warm June morning. She held tightly on to my arm, leaning her body against mine, and I realized she was in the middle of having a Ménière's attack, obviously brought on by the pressure of performing.

She was too unsteady to go much farther than the Starbucks next door. I helped her to a table and got in line for two coffees and chocolate cookies.

"I'll be all right," she said as I placed a coffee and cookie before her. "I just took a Dramamine; that sometimes helps a little."

I asked her how the commercial went.

"I've no idea. Most of my effort was in trying to keep my bearings. Won't see it until it plays on TV. But the director didn't seem unhappy."

"What was it about?"

She laughed. "I'm an ooh-la-la princess, luxuriously surrounded, with three kneeling knights before me, each proffering a fancy bottle of perfume. I sniff bottle one and reject him, then reject number two as well, but I'm ecstatic over three's perfume, which happens to be—surprise!—my sponsor's bottle. What wore me down was having to do so many takes, repeat, repeat, thanks to poopy suitor two."

I asked her if she would like to do more commercials. That brought a long sigh out of her. "What I'd like," she said finally, "is another coffee."

CHAPTER TWENTY-THREE

It was a small, neglected courtroom that had only a residue of the grandiosity of the still-impressive courthouse at 60 Centre Street: dated wood paneling, faded velvet curtains, eight rows of benches, a stale pervasive odor left by antiseptic mops.

It was a six-person jury: four men, two women. During the voir dire jury selection, a streaker had disrupted the courtroom and the cops had had the damnedest time apprehending him. The good news was it wasn't my syndrome—this time. The bad news was that the nude spectacle had made it hard to get a feel for the jury members.

Shore and Norgaard sat at the plaintiff's table on the right side of the room, next to the jury. She was clad in a black three-piece pin-striped Hugo Boss power suit that put my sensible Brooks Brothers wool suit to shame. A retinue of junior associates filled the first row of the gallery behind Shore.

On the bride's side of the aisle, I sat at the defendant's table with Penelope and Charlie. Lois was positioned directly behind me with a pile of documents at the ready. The gallery was nearly full, a mix of court watchers and members of the press. Scanning the crowd, I was heartened to find Emma seated in the back. Assuming that she was real, it felt good to have the support. The night before she had done her best to encourage me, letting me run my opening argument by her and giving me gentle notes on performance. Syndrome fake or not, her presence was certainly a boon to my morale.

The bailiff cleared his throat.

"All rise!"

Judge Peter McArdle strode into the courtroom and took a seat. A dignified jurist in his late sixties, he was firm but fair with lawyers but was known for being quite gentle with witnesses and juries.

"You may be seated. Is plaintiff's counsel prepared for opening remarks?"

"Yes, Your Honor."

Shore began: "Ladies and gentlemen of the jury, this is a simple case. My client Daniel Norgaard is an esteemed poet and a man of high moral character. Yet, for the sin of falling out of love, Ms. Tee has maliciously maligned his character and vandalized his art, all for the sake of drumming up interest in her tacky book. Just because *Topiary* is a work of fiction does not entitle Ms. Tee to make up facts. Worse yet, Miss Victoria Celluci has also been smeared. What did she ever do to Penelope Tee? She's just collateral damage in Ms. Tee's heinous attack."

I watched the jury as Shore monologued, trying to read their faces for signals about the way they might be leaning. Because this was a civil trial, neither side needed all six jurors: New York allows a non-unanimous verdict if five out of six agree. That meant if I could identify one holdout based on body language, the best thing to do was to ignore them and focus on the other five. Juror 1, the foreman—a bald, bearded chiropractor in a plaid button-down and khakis—was attentive and scribbling notes. He had served on a jury before and knew the drill. Juror 3, a fratty college student—was his name Chad?—with an unruly mop of wavy curls and a striped rugby shirt, was staring a hole through his Converse sneakers. Was Chad/3 indifferent, hungover, or both? As a precaution, I jotted down a quick sketch of each juror and quietly slid it to Charlie with a note: "which 1s = real?" Charlie put check marks next to all six jurors and gave me a thumbs-up under the table.

Shore continued. "The testimony you will hear today will prove that Ms. Tee knowingly lied about an affair and subjected my client to immense damages—reputational and emotional. Further, we'll prove that Ms. Tee stole Mr. Norgaard's poem. She is nothing more than a graffiti artist, tagging her name on top of someone else's art. She calls it her art. Well, here in a court of law we call that copyright infringement. I thank you all in advance for your time and consideration."

"Counsel for defendant?"

I stood up, closed my eyes tight for a moment, and took a deep breath. When I opened them, there were extra jurors in the box—ten in all.

After a lurch of despair, I began to feel an angry rise of resentment, like I used to feel in my college basketball days when the opposition swarmed me to stifle my scoring. Instead of focusing on winning five, now I would need to convince nine. I could feel my body growing taut. I tried to steal a quick glance at my seating chart to remind myself which were real, but there was a large ficus sitting on the table on top of it. So I took one more breath and tried to push the feeling of dread down into some deep recess of my body.

"Good morning. I'm sure you all found my opposing counsel's remarks quite . . . spirited. But I would be remiss not to remind you that underlying the disputed facts in this case is a very important tenet of our constitutional rights—freedom of speech. I humbly ask you as jurors to keep that in mind as the plaintiff attempts to denigrate Penelope Tee's art. Oh, and by the way, Danny Norgaard did cheat on my client. Ms. Tee could have spoken to the tabloid press the way Danny Norgaard did, feeding them story after story. Instead she chose to let her art speak for itself. There's nothing tawdry about that at all. You know, there are two types of novelists—those who write about themselves and those who pretend not to."

A couple of the jurors smiled and nodded. I was pretty sure they were real because I remembered them from voir dire when we first empaneled the jury.

"So, at bottom, Danny Norgaard not only wants to be able to treat women as disposable, he wants to make sure that he owns their stories too."

Juror 5—a bouncer at a nightclub who'd said during voir dire that his sister wrote poetry—perked up and scribbled something on his notepad while the vaudeville clown next to him dozed off, his head resting on his fellow juror's broad shoulders.

"Not only that, he wants the world to know that his opus 'Cacio e Pepe' is off-limits. Hands off. Don't touch his precious masterpiece. Last time I checked, there was something called the First Amendment. The First Amendment is number one in the Constitution and in my heart, because without it the Danny Norgaards of the world get to tell us what to say, to write, to paint, to create. The testimony you'll hear today will show you that Penelope Tee is a truth teller and artist. I thank you as well for stepping up as citizens to uphold the rule of law."

"Thank you, counselor," said Judge McArdle. "Ms. Shore, who is your first witness?"

"Mr. Norgaard, Your Honor."

Shore teed them up and Norgaard knocked them out. He was a stand-up guy, had always tried to do right by Penelope but nothing was ever enough. When he left, he tried to be classy about it. Once *Topiary* came out, it was humiliating. Publishers were backing off from signing him; a promising fellowship evaporated. He felt the chill of longtime friends icing him out. And then to top it all, he had to see his magnum opus turned into a poop joke. Norgaard teared up at that last part—possibly genuinely. I would have to be careful on cross-examination.

"Mr. Norgaard, is it true you are currently dating Ms. Celluci?"

"Yes, it's true. What's wrong with that?"

"Respectfully, I'm asking the questions." The cowboy on his horse standing next to the witness box tilted his hat and gave me a wink. I started to shoo him but managed to catch myself and pulled my hand toward my hair, mussing it back like I was a kid whose high-five had gone unrequited and had to play it off smoothly.

"And how long have you known one another?"

"Oh, going on three years now."

"How do you know each other?"

"Penelope hired her for a shrub consultation at my summer house in the Hamptons. We knew a lot of people in common and the three of us became friends."

"And when did the relationship turn romantic?"

"Look, I'm not going to deny there was chemistry from

the beginning, but I'm a gentleman and I was committed to making it work with Penelope. It wasn't until the relationship ended several months later that I asked out Victoria."

"Do you recall which day you broke it off?"

"I remember waiting until after New Year's because I didn't want to ruin her holiday."

"And when was your first date with Ms. Celluci?"

"I didn't tell Victoria how I felt until a few weeks after that."

"So there was no overlap between your romantic relationships with Ms. Celluci and Ms. Tee?"

"It was strictly platonic."

"All business?"

"Objection, asked and answered," said Shore.

"Withdrawn. I'm introducing a photograph of Mr. Norgaard and Ms. Celluci, appearing in the *New York Post.*"

"Go ahead, we'll mark it Exhibit One," said the judge.

"Do you recognize this photo?"

"Yeah, this is the pap photo taken of me and Victoria, maybe six months before my breakup with Penelope. I was in LA for a reading, she was there getting some custom pruning shears, and we grabbed dinner."

"Was it a date?"

"Of course not."

"Objection, asked and answered," Shore interjected once more.

"Overruled, but do try to get to your point," Judge McArdle admonished me.

"Can you read the caption for me?"

" 'Pretty-boy poet Danny Norgaard cozies up'—this is ridiculous."

"Please finish."

"'Cozies up to tree trimmer to the stars Victoria Celluci over a romantic plate of pasta at chic hotspot Chi Spacca.'"

"Sounds romantic, no?"

"It's typical tabloid bullshit."

Judge McArdle cleared his throat. Bouncer/juror 5 chuckled while number 4—a schoolteacher who wore a diamond cross—rolled her eyes.

"Excuse me—tabloid . . . garbage. Victoria was raving about the penne and that I had to try it, so I slid over to her side of the booth—for a second!—and had a bite. That's cozy?"

"Look, the heart wants what it wants."

"Objection!"

"Counselor, is there a question?"

"I suppose the question is, do you really expect us to believe there was nothing hinky going on?"

A hush fell over the courtroom. I turned around and saw Charlie and Lois steal an "oh no you didn't" glance at each other. Among the jury, Spider-Man seemed particularly impressed, though his expressions were hard to read behind his mask. Although juror—was it 2?—was vigorously shaking his head. Uh-oh. Maybe he was a misogynist.

"Objection, argumentative."

"Sustained. The jury will disregard Mr. Tremaine's previous question."

Number 2/vigorous head-shaker was staring daggers at me. Only now, on his right side, an identical double of the man was doing the same.

"Apologies, Your Honor. I'll move on. Mr. Norgaard, do you recall what you were eating that night?"

"Objection—relevance."

"Counselor?"

"The relevance will be apparent soon. Scout's honor."

"Objection overruled."

"Well, then objection, asked and answered. He said it was penne."

"Counselor?"

"The penne he referred to was Ms. Celluci's."

Judge McArdle sighed. "Is it important that we know what shape everyone's pasta was?"

"It is."

"Oh, what the heck. Objection overruled. But if I hear a question about which sorbet he ordered I'm holding you in contempt."

"Thank you, Judge. Mr. Norgaard—the question was, what kind of pasta did you eat that evening?"

"I don't recall. I'm partial to their lasagna."

"But you're certain Ms. Celluci had penne?"

"Not one hundred percent, no."

"Okay, in that case, I'm going to introduce some evidence that might refresh your memory. This is a copy of the menu from the evening in question, attached with an affidavit from Chef Nancy Silverton authenticating it."

Norgaard turned beet red. Shore jumped out of her seat. "Objection!"

Judge McArdle was exasperated. "You're objecting to a pasta menu?"

"Uh, no, Your Honor. Withdrawn with apologies."

I returned to my cross-examination. "Can you read for me the menu?"

Norgaard put on his reading glasses. "It says it's a special Memorial Day menu, with a couples' prix fixe of Caesar salad, *cacio e pepe*, and lemon sorbet . . ." His voice trailed off.

"I'm sorry, I couldn't hear that. Did you say *cacio e pepe*?"

Norgaard looked like he'd just bitten into a lemon, and soon would be forced to eat the rest of the tree.

"Ahem . . . I did. I guess I forgot that was on the menu."

"The couples' menu?"

"Er . . . yes."

"What a coincidence. Isn't 'Cacio e Pepe' the title of your magnum opus?"

"I wouldn't use those words, but *Poet's Digest* did call it that."

"What inspired you to write this poem?"

"Well, if you must know, I wrote it for Penelope. So you can imagine how I feel seeing it defaced like that."

"That's sweet. When did you publish the poem?"

"It was part of my latest anthology, *Dickin-son*, which came out two years ago."

"So after the cozy dinner but before the breakup."

"Yeah—I mean, no. I mean, yes, it was in between those dates. I mean, it was in that specific time period. But I didn't get cozy."

A single bead of sweat dripped down Norgaard's brow.

"No further questions."

When I sat back down at the defense table, I could feel the buzz in the courtroom. Charlie nudged me and whispered, "Great job making him admit to eating couples' pasta, but where exactly are you going with this?"

"You'll see."

Next up Shore called Celluci as a witness. Celluci insisted she had great respect for Penelope and would never make a move on someone who was taken.

Now it was my turn.

"Ms. Cespuglio . . . excuse me, Celluci. Mr. Norgaard

says he kept things strictly platonic until after the breakup. Is that true?"

"*Naturalmente.* Of course."

"Let's talk for a moment about 'Cacio e Pepe.' Mr. Norgaard says he wrote it for Ms. Tee. How does it feel to be dating someone whose most famous work is dedicated to the ex-girlfriend you replaced?"

"*Bene.* It's . . . like you said. Sweet." Celluci played it cool but I could tell I had struck a nerve.

"It really is. You see, Penelope was his muse, his source of inspiration. I confess, I've recently been struck by Cupid's arrow."

Shore rolled her eyes. "Objection—relevance?"

Judge McArdle smiled. "I'm a little lost too, but let's see where this goes."

"I'm in love with a woman named Emma. She's sitting in the gallery here today."

I spared a glance, afraid of what I would see—or not see. But Emma was there, smiling through her blushes.

"She gives me strength. I feel like a better man because of her. If I could dedicate my own legal writing to someone, it would be her. Would you say you make Mr. Norgaard feel that way?"

Celluci smiled broadly. "Of course!"

It was time to lay my trap.

"I call Emma my queen." This was a small falsehood, but I couldn't tell six to ten real and imaginary jurors that in my heart my love bore the affectionate name of "Sleeve Lady." "What's your nickname for each other?"

"I call him Mio Re, 'My King.' He calls me La Bella."

She had answered so quickly, she hadn't bothered to look

at the plaintiff's table, where Norgaard was staring a hole through her head. And just like that, I had snared my unsuspecting prey. I signaled to Lois, who tossed me a copy of Norgaard's book.

"La Bella? That's so sweet. Say, could you do me a favor? Read the dedication page for *Dickin-son*. I'm introducing it as Exhibit Three."

" 'To my . . . bella.' "

"That's funny, I didn't realize he called Penelope the same thing. Does it bother you to share a nickname?"

Something broke inside Celluci. Her façade instantly melted.

"*Che cazzo!* I am the muse, his inspiration! This idiot did not know what she had. 'Cacio e Pepe' was written for me!"

"Objection!"

"What for?"

"I don't know, Your Honor!"

"No further questions."

When I returned to my table, I dared another look at the gallery. Emma's eyes were shining: an embracing look of pride, love, commitment.

I knew I had Norgaard dead to rights on the affair. But what would the jury make of the copyright infringement? At summation, I went all in on the power of love.

"Ladies and gentlemen of the jury. The testimony you heard today proved, conclusively, that my client was the one who was wronged. Viewed through the lens of a discarded muse, the meaning of 'Cacca e Pipì' is abundantly clear. It is a statement on how not all love is forever. No, not everyone gets to be that lucky. Penelope Tee has revealed to the world how empty Daniel Norgaard's platitudes about love and devotion are, and in doing so has transformed the entire meaning of the work. Therefore I urge you all to return a verdict of fair use. Thank you."

There was silence for a moment; then the courtroom erupted into a furor of chatter. I walked past the defense table and made a direct line to Emma, who had come down from the gallery to meet me. She put her arms around me and touched my lips with hers.

"Thank *you*," I said.

"For what?"

"Making me do what I just did."

"Me?"

"Yes, you. I couldn't have done it without you."

"I feel the same," she said.

Even buoyed as I was by her presence, I felt the need for realism. "I may still lose, you know."

"No, as far as I'm concerned, you've already won."

An amused Judge McArdle—I'd read him correctly as a man who enjoyed a good spectacle—waited a few minutes before restoring order. Then he thanked the jury for paying close attention and told them the moment had come for them to decide the case.

"You have an important responsibility here, and one I urge you not to take lightly. So take as much time as you need, and please go into your deliberations with an open mind. Try to listen to each other and to reach a unanimous verdict. It's getting close to five p.m. here so we can reconvene tomorrow at nine a.m."

The jurors dutifully nodded, except for Vaudeville, who honked his nose. As they filed out, I noted that the syndrome fakers were disappearing and not going into the jury room. *Both* vigorous head-shakers were among the fakes, which seemed to improve my odds.

CHAPTER TWENTY-FOUR

As I replayed the trial in my head that evening, I knew I had knocked out the defamation claim. The copyright claim was anybody's ball game—even assholes deserve protection. But essentially, win or lose, I felt good that I had overcome my obeisance to the syndrome fakers. And how had I overcome it? With Emma's urging. With the insightful care she showed me, just as I cared for her. The smile that greeted me at the end of my summation, her embrace, her involvement. And mine in her life. I felt no small sense of pride that I'd had a role in liberating her from her fear of not being able to free herself from her Ménière's imprisonment.

The next morning I got to the courthouse in time to snag a coffee and a croissant. I'd fed Bhairav generous helpings of wine and blood and presented a rose to Kishani before leaving the apartment. I felt good—or as good as I ever felt before a judgment.

Judge McArdle summoned the jury.

"Do you have a verdict?"

The foreman answered: "We're close, Judge. But can you clarify one more time what malice means?"

"Certainly. Don't think of that word in the common parlance. You can have malice in your heart without it infecting your head. If you feel Ms. Tee was wrong in her assertion that infidelity occurred, then you have to decide whether she was simply mistaken or not."

It was not a great sign that the jury was talking about malice, because that tended to indicate that the truth defense had failed. But I knew better than to make assumptions.

For me, waiting for a jury decision is the most tedious and exasperating aspect of being a lawyer. And so it was that morning. I had brought one of P. G. Wodehouse's Jeeves books, with its wonderfully amusing account of life in the twenties narrated by that bumbling upper-class British twit Bertie Wooster, but not even that, try as I did, could distract me from the impending verdict.

At eleven a.m. the judge brought in the jury and inquired once again whether they were close to a verdict. The foreman answered, "Not yet, Your Honor, we're real close though."

"Try to wrap it up before lunch if you can."

Charlie phoned me and so did Emma, but both calls were brief because the courtroom frowned upon the use of cell phones, so I had to take the calls outside. Lois came by with checks for me to sign, but other than that the afternoon droned on with nary a peep from the jury room. At the plaintiff's table there was only one junior lawyer keeping vigil. I made a couple of attempts to involve myself with Jeeves and Bertie, but not even the great Wodehouse could distract me.

At one o'clock, as I was returning from the men's room, the red light outside the jury room came to life and the bailiff went into the judge's chambers to inform him that the jury wished to return. They filed into the jury box as he returned to the bench. The bailiff announced that the court was in session and Judge McArdle rapped his gavel.

"Okay, let's try this again, hopefully for the last time. Have you reached a verdict?"

The foreman stood up. "Yes, Your Honor."

"What is your verdict?"

He handed the signed verdict paper to the bailiff, who handed it to the judge, who unfolded it and read: " 'We were not able to reach unanimity but five of us find the defendant not liable on both counts.' " The college frat boy looked down at his shoes and the others side-eyed him. All this trouble just to try to get him to join a unanimous verdict?

The judge thanked the jury and discharged them. I stood frozen in my tracks. I couldn't believe it: I had done it.

Everyone on our side was demonstratively elated with the verdict. Emma exuded delight, Penelope vowed to dedicate her next book to me (no thank you), and when Charlie called Flakfizer to tell her Norgaard would be on the hook for much of Dodecahedron's legal fees, she was positively giddy.

Charlie insisted on a celebration in Connecticut over the weekend, including Emma. But Emma was not so sure. I told her that there was a nice guest room with good art on the walls, but she said, "That's fine, but how far from the city is your place?"

"About an hour, bit more on weekends. But you've got pills and the stick-on to put behind your ear, haven't you?"

"That's for air travel, to deal with the cabin pressure as it vacillates during flight. But, listen, we both have to take chances. You took the chance that you could manage this trial. I think it's my turn. Yes, I'd adore going to Connecticut and taking my chances that I can survive the turbulence and celebrate your victory."

"*Our* victory. You goaded me into it."

My blind eye forbidding me to drive, my occasional driver and helper since the invasion of the syndrome, Ronnie, picked me up in my Subaru and, in deference to Emma, drove at a steady pace in the heavy Friday traffic. I called ahead to have a pickup dinner waiting for us at Tarry Lodge restaurant. I was excited at the prospect of having Emma for the weekend, on top of my excitement over the verdict in the courtroom.

Emma was effusively delighted with my cottage: its hominess, its deep fireplace, its quaint country kitchen, the koi-inhabited pool, and especially the sweeping view, with its deep-green surroundings. Of course, the syndrome still had its high rickety fence covering my experience of the view, but Emma saw none of that. She loved the guest room with its emphasis on art I had collected. No Mirós or Matisses, just new paintings I had discovered, prowling the little art shops in Greenwich Village. I found having Emma with me in this favorite empowering place of mine exhilarating, somehow mysteriously illuminating some of my dark unfilled niches.

I have a flagstone terrace that runs across the entire breadth of the cottage, and that's where we had dinner, lighted by two hurricane lamps. I uncorked a bottle of Sancerre to have with the gorgonzola salad, and a Chianti for the Bolognese that I warmed up in the microwave.

After dinner we adjourned to the double chairs on the terrace, where we sipped more Chianti and chatted—about what, I can't recall, but we laughed and teased one another and had a fine time.

When it became quite late, I reluctantly walked her to her bedroom, where I made sure she had everything she needed.

She had suffered a full attack of vertigo that had lasted a couple of hours when she got out of the car at the end of the drive from New York, but for the most part she was pleased with her reaction to the journey, and so was I.

We hugged each other as we said good night, her body pressed close to mine. We exchanged a long smiling look.

I closed the door and returned to the terrace, wanting to think about the events of this extraordinary day. I thought about the cottage and how Emma's presence had emphasized its full appeal. I had bought it soon after I started to practice law. An elderly real estate broker named Mabel Frost had shown me around the area, where I wanted to buy a place to be near Charlie, but I soon realized that this cottage, then completely run-down and in need of extensive inside and outside restoration, was the only thing I could afford. As my practice grew, so grew the cottage. And so did the koi I got FedExed from Tricker's Water Lilies and Fishes in Independence, Ohio, which I raised in the little rectangular reflecting pool I installed in the middle of my lawn. In the beginning a few guests and girlfriends visited, but for a long time now I had preferred being alone to enjoy music, work on office problems, and occasionally make slow progress writing the next book in my mystery series. There had been one woman I was serious about, a lovely girl who wrote content for a greeting card company, but she was spirited away by the Hollywood lure of a competitive company. And now all these years later, including the abysmal time with Violet, there was Emma. I unwrapped one of my Cuban cigars and thought about Emma. Thought deeply about Emma.

I awoke with the first vestiges of dawn. The wine bottle was empty. My half-smoked cigar was on the flagstone beside my chaise. I pulled myself up and stretched my stiff neck. I pitched the bottle and cigar into the waste receptacle in the kitchen, and on my way to my bedroom I glanced at Emma's closed door. It was an uplifting feeling, having her there, so close.

CHAPTER TWENTY-FIVE

After retiring to my room, I awoke again at a more civilized hour to the welcome aroma of coffee. I donned my terry-cloth robe and found Emma on the terrace with a mug and *The New York Times*.

"There was a bag with croissants and bagels from the Main Street Bakery next to the *Times*. They're warming in the oven."

I laughed. "Looks like I'm the guest, not you."

"Yep, I am *not* a guest. I don't know what I am, but, well, it's something else."

I went to the kitchen and put the warm croissants and bagels on plates, along with butter, blackberry jelly, and cream cheese. Emma had followed me and took care of the coffee. We set up everything on the terrace and spent a leisurely morning slathering croissants and bagels and sharing dismal news from the *Times*.

"Why must everything be so awful?" she asked.

"You mean they should just write about happy people who are enjoying life?"

"Why not? Or at least lay off the crummy politicians."

"Nobody would read it. Readers like hearing about the comeuppance of foul people and destructive events."

I took Emma for a walk along the narrow road that ran by the cottage and led to a white-steepled Colonial church and cemetery. We walked among the old tombstones with names and inscriptions dating back to Revolutionary times.

For brunch I fired up the griddle while Emma brewed a pot of tea and set a lovely table for us, enhanced with flowers from the garden. She sang snatches of a lovely Shakespearean song while she cut the flowers and arranged them delicately on the terrace table.

"The forward violet thus did I chide:
Sweet thief, whence didst thou steal thy sweet that smells,
If not from my love's breath? The purple pride
Which on thy soft cheek for complexion dwells
In my love's veins thou hast too grossly dy'd.
The lily I condemned for thy hand,
And buds of marjoram had stol'n thy hair;
The roses fearfully on thorns did stand,
One blushing shame, another white despair . . ."

I filled our plates with spatula'd pancakes pregnant with blueberries. We sat facing each other while I asked Alexa to play Alfred Brendel at the piano. We passed the maple syrup back and forth and I had the illusion I had somehow stumbled my way through the heavenly gate with the angel Emma waiting for me, accompanied by Brendel's ethereal piano.

———

Charlie and Lydia had invited us for an afternoon at their pool followed by dinner. Their spacious house was on a rise over the sound with a section of beach beneath, but they preferred their commodious pool, which had been built to their liking, along with a small bathhouse, all of it a testament to Charlie's rise to junior partner at his high-decibel law firm.

Naturally young Alfred was the star attraction, but Emma captured Lydia as well as Charlie. There was a baby nurse, Miss Vivika ("only for the first month," Charlie said), which freed up Lydia. Late in the afternoon, there was an incident at the swimming pool that shook us up. Charlie and I were engaged in some very competitive gin rummy, Lydia had gone into the house to breastfeed the baby, and Emma was sitting on a floating chair reading one of my detective books. While Charlie studied his hand I glanced over at Emma, but her chair had turned on its side; my book was floating and she was not. I jumped up, spilling the cards all over, and dived into the pool, Charlie following me. I spotted Emma struggling near the bottom and, putting my arm around her, brought her to the surface. She was coughing and trying to inhale.

Charlie spread a beach towel on the ground. I put her on her stomach and started to push down on her back.

"I'm all right," she managed to say between coughs that brought up pool water. "Tried to come out . . . chair turned over and . . . I went wobbly . . . my head spinning . . . swallowed some water . . ."

"No charge," Charlie said, a slightly hysterical edge to his laugh. I realized I was shaking all over, trembling worse than Emma.

She was now sitting up as the cough cured itself. Charlie offered her a Coke. She took it gladly, and though I knew she wouldn't want me hovering or treating her like glass, I went with her to occupy a commodious deck chair. Lydia joined us with Alfred in her arms.

"What did I miss?" she asked.

"I did my world-famous water performance."

"Her swim song," I said, deciding to follow her lead in the attitude we were displaying toward all of this. She squeezed my hand in appreciation.

"Pity," an oblivious Lydia said.

Alfred made no comment but he swung my silver rattle in his chubby little fist.

In not too long, we shook off the scare and our appetites returned. We had a lovely dinner of gazpacho, goat cheese salad with Bibb lettuce, and lobster thermidor accompanied by Baron de L, an elite in the hierarchy of white wine.

Charlie held up his glass for a toast. "Here's to you, Chet. It took real courage to face that jury and risk failure. Here's to you, my great, great friend, my brother."

After dinner, the ladies discovered a surprising affinity for performing together at the piano and they created a four-handed version of songs from *West Side Story* to *My Fair Lady*, their voices providing them with natural harmony. There was no doubt that Emma Vicky had been received with open arms and perhaps hearts.

It was late when we returned to the cottage. Dark clouds were sliding over the moon but I suggested a few minutes on the terrace before retiring. The north wind was starting to pick up strength. I brought sambucas and a jacket for Emma to the terrace. We toasted each other as a light rain began to fall on our canvas roof.

"What heaven," Emma said as she sipped her sambuca. "I love the thrumming of falling rain, don't you?"

We sat for a while, holding hands, sipping our drinks, and listening to the rain.

When the mantel clock struck the hour we roused ourselves and went inside.

"Today was lovely, Chet."

"Yes, and so are you."

We hugged and she disappeared into her room.

I turned off the lights.

CHAPTER TWENTY-SIX

The electrical storm struck with a fierceness I had never experienced. It announced itself with a deafening slam of thunder that shook the cottage, accompanied by a blast of lightning that struck very close nearby and painted the night white with its intensity. One after the other, in quick succession, shards of lightning stabbed around the cottage. The fierceness of the wind was upending things on the terrace. The sound of tables and chairs scudding across flagstones, glass breaking, doors banging, the entire cottage under siege by the unceasing lightning. My door flew open, and Emma ran into the room, desperately calling my name, throwing herself into my bed, into my arms, grabbing at me with frightened panic. At first she seemed simply to be burying her hysteria in my chest, but then her purpose changed, and with cries that accompanied the peak peals of thunder, we fell into the coupling that seemed inevitable, our climaxes fueled by the storm's. Some syndrome people sprang up in the bed watching us, a momentary interruption, but the intensity of my desire overcame them, and when the storm began slowly to abate, so too did we subside, locked in each other's arms, to resume the night together.

It was just past noon when we awoke, still embracing, facing each other; we smiled and she pushed my hair away from my eyes. "Are you all right?" she asked in a whispery voice. I looked into her gold-flecked eyes, closely perched on the bridge of my nose. In those eyes I saw something I had never dreamed would be directed at me. My arms responded by tightening around her as she rolled over me and we prolonged what we had found in the stormy night.

We put on our robes and went out to look at the storm's mayhem. Armed with cups of coffee and toasted muffins, we picked our way around all the fallen objects and upended reclining chairs, tables, and plants. The grounds were covered with broken branches and leaves, and the terrace was unrecognizable. We sat at the table with our muffins and coffees and surveyed the damage, which Ronnie would attend to later with his tractor and chipper.

We made our way out to the pond to check on the koi. The surface was heavily littered but the fish were fine and came to us at a clear place, where we fed them. We sat on one of the stone benches that faced the pool. I assumed my meditative position and Emma followed, holding my hand. "Remember, Emmy, the monks told me we are a cosmic flower," I said. "And chanting om is opening the 'psychic petals of that flower to all the love in the universe.'"

We chanted om for a good half hour, eyes shut, faces to the sky. I tried to straighten out the tangle of my mind but it resisted. Nevertheless, om was reassuring. I glanced at Emma and wondered if she was doing any better. Her upturned face was truly beautiful but her placid chant gave no indication of whether she was "sorting things out" any better than I was. "Sorting things out." What a meaningless cliché. And yet, I wished that the spirit of my om could help me have a clear view of where to go and what to do.

Charlie had suggested we drive back to New York with him and that we leave in the late afternoon to avoid the dense returning weekenders. Lydia would come with Alfred later in the week. We put Emma in the backseat where she could stretch out with her head on a pillow to minimize the possible effects of the journey on her Ménière's. Charlie played Chet Baker on his Sirius radio while he and I softly discussed legal matters.

When we reached Emma's apartment building, the afternoon was giving way to evening. As I helped her from the car I found her very unsteady, having to cling to my arm to keep her balance. The doorman took her overnight bag, and we thanked Charlie for the ride and all the rest.

"Chet," Emma said, "can we sit here on this bench for a while? I can't face the elevator just yet. Vertigo is rearing its dismal head."

There were bushes on each side of the bench, which was just across from the building's entrance, a modest maple tree above it. Emma closed her eyes and clutched my arm firmly, leaning her head against my shoulder. There were a few people on the footpaths but no one paid any attention to us.

"I guess the commuting process is too much for you," I said.

"Oh no, it's a *prohcess* I'll get used to."

To lighten things up, I sang, "You say *prohcess* and I say *prahcess*, you say *nyther* and I say *neether*," and we began to giggle.

Chet: "You like *patahto* and I like *potato*."

Emma: "You like *tomato* and I like *tomahto*."

Chet: "You say *lahfter* and I say *laffter*."

Emma: "You like *pajammas*, I like *pahjahmas*."

Chet: "I say *father* and you say *pater*."

Emma: "You say *mother* and I say *mater*."

Chet: "*Mother, mater.*"

Emma: "*Bananas, banahnas.*"

Chet: "Let's call the whole thing off. Then we must part . . ."

Emma: "If we must part, then that would break my heart . . ."

She burst into tears and threw herself into my arms.

I tried to comfort her. "Oh, Emmy, listen, it's only a silly song."

She pulled back and looked at me through her tears. "I'll do eether and neether and tomaytoes and laffter and bananas and . . ."

I pulled her back against me. "Don't you dare. We must keep you just as you are . . . We are."

"But you don't understand, Chet, I love you. From the very first, love, love, love you, and now it's bad. Really really bad . . ."

"And I love you, Emmy, *eyether* and all. Give us a little time—we've been struck by lightning, don't forget, all over."

I carried her bag up to her apartment and the lightning struck again where it had left off.

CHAPTER TWENTY-SEVEN

I was at a loss trying desperately to choose between what I wanted to do impetuously and what was probably better and more sensible for us. I truly loved Emma, and no matter what we decided I wanted her to prosper despite whatever drawbacks the decision inflicted on her. I didn't want her sudden impulses, and mine, to overcome that old standby— reason. I phoned the office of my old family doctor, Dr. Litman, in Brooklyn for an immediate appointment, but they said he was fully booked for the next five days. Even though he sometimes smoked a cigar during a session and often dozed off, the ash tumbling down onto his vest, his devoted patients tolerated all his idiosyncrasies.

When Doc Lou called me back later I kidded him for maintaining a full schedule at eighty-eight years of age.

"You're right, you're right, but I'm going with an eighty-two-year-old chick now and I want to look like I can still carry a load. She still carries her load as a contralto at the Met." He cleared his throat. "Is it urgent, Chet, or something that can—"

"Urgent."

"About your Bonnet syndrome?"

"And then some. Please? It's a kind of crisis."

Although technically an internist, he practiced physical medicine with related psychiatric advice and prescriptions. He was also ordained and occasionally married his clients.

"Okay, Chet, tell you what—how about dinner tonight?"

I met him at seven o'clock at a restaurant in Brooklyn. He arrived on time, jaunty as usual, in a three-piece beige linen suit with a red silk handkerchief flapped over the top of his suit pocket.

"Do you mind eating kosher? My wife, Ina, loved it here— they treat me like I'm King Solomon."

A bottle of wine arrived, poured by a waiter wearing a white apron down to his ankles. Doc Lou ordered for both of us and raised his glass to me.

"You're not in trouble with the law, are you?"

"Not at all."

"Fine. *L'chaim.*"

I'd never had a kosher wine; this one was a red—a bit sweet, but I liked it. Bowls of borscht arrived with little tuffets of sour cream floating on the surface.

· "All right, Chetsky, let's hear the troubles."

In between spoons of delicious beet soup, I took Doc Lou through the Emma saga. As the main course of mushroom-stuffed cabbage and latkes was put before us, he drew me out with questions, mostly about how I would respond to certain situations.

"The way I see it," he said, "you are truly in deep love with this splendid young woman whom you would like to keep in your life. She, meanwhile, would like to keep you in hers, but with your serious handicaps, are you putting yourselves in jeopardy? And if you do stay together, would you live together unmarried or married, or live apart but see each other, or is it best to break up, even though it would be very painful? First off, let me tell you my own dilemma way back. I met Ina in med school and we were in love as you are in love. My father was a good fellow who had a small store that sold rare books. He was an Orthodox Jew. Her father was the head of a large investment company and the head of the congregation of his Catholic church. Ina and I wanted to marry before we left med school but both fathers sternly forbade it. Ina's dad threatened to disown her, and when we did marry, as threatened, he never saw her again: he disinherited her, never met our children. My father was not as severe, but although Ina went through the ritual of converting, my father and mother never socialized with us or our kids. Ina's old man even forbade Ina from attending his funeral. Of course, you don't have that kind of parental opposition, but I tell you about Ina and me as an illustration of what sacrifices have to be made. For example, her Ménière's can make pregnancy difficult."

"Is it hereditary?"

"I don't think so, but I once had a patient who had Ménière's and every time she got pregnant, some physical upheaval would cause a miscarriage. But she wouldn't give up. Decided to spend the entire nine months in bed, not moving at all. Didn't work. In her eighth month she had a miscarriage. In bed."

A dessert of warm apple strudel with vanilla ice cream arrived. The topic had not done anything for my appetite, but then I tasted it and immediately surrendered.

"On the other hand," Doc Lou was saying, "my friend Dr.

Vinegarde had a forty-year-old Ménière's patient who had never previously been able to conceive, then produced for her and her amazed hubby healthy twin boys. Simply put, Chet, it's trusting in the unknown, but I say either go for it or forget it—drink of the lusty wine or spurn the glass."

It was good advice, and it might once have sealed the deal for me. But now there was a spiritual Nepali influence I'd introduced into my life that had to be considered: the words and attitude of Dr. Gopal and the impact of Karki and his drums, bells, and chants. So I sat down with Bhairav to listen to myself, and one totally unexpected suggestion came flowing back to me: what if, yes, what if my reunion with Emma was somehow influenced by the spirits contacted by Karki in that water buffalo ceremony in Durbar Square?

CHAPTER TWENTY-EIGHT

I checked the time: eleven thirty. I went to the fridge and took out a split of Dom Pérignon champagne and two flutes. I put them in Bhairav's carry bag, though I left behind Bhairav himself. My heart was racing with anticipation, as if I were going to try to rob a bank.

The bag and I went downstairs, hailed a cab to take us to Gramercy Park. I waved to Viktor, the doorman, who was well acquainted with me by now, and I took the elevator up to Emma's apartment. Using the key she had recently given me, I quietly opened the door. A crooked-nosed reading lamp illuminated an empty chair with an open book on its cushion. Soft music was playing from an Amazon cylinder.

Two arms suddenly grabbed me from behind, wrapping around me and rattling the glass in my bag. I let out a surprised "Whoa!" as the voice from behind, unmistakably Emma trying to sound tough, barked, "Don't move!"

I exploded with a woof of mirth.

"I have a question you've got to answer!" Emma demanded, still tough.

"Okay."

"Chet Tremaine, will you please marry me?"

I busted with laughter. "That's what I came to ask . . ."

"I beat you to it."

"How did you know?" I couldn't stop, the joy kept spilling out.

"Answer the question!"

"Yes, yes, I will marry you." I twisted from her grasp and got on a knee in front of her. "Emma Vicky, will you please marry *me*?"

She threw herself on me, knocking both of us into a heap on the floor.

"Yes!" she said, after we untangled ourselves. "Yes! Yes! Yes!" She threw her arms around my neck and planted a ferocious kiss on my lips. "Till death do us part?"

"Let's not get ahead of ourselves." I reached in my bag and took out the Dom Pérignon, which I opened with a lusty pop and a bit of flow as I filled the two flutes. We extended the flutes toward each other, the golden bubbles dancing before us, and we both grew quiet; more than quiet—contemplative.

"I truly love you, Chet. Now and forever."

"And I love you, Emma, beyond eternity."

We finished the champagne.

CHAPTER TWENTY-NINE

Emma and I had planned to have a quiet wedding at the clerk's office at city hall with Charlie and Lydia as witnesses, but Charlie would have none of it.

"We're going to have the wedding at our Connecticut place," he insisted. "It's my birthright—after all that I put up with it's the least you could do to repay me."

And so it came to pass that embossed wedding invitations were sent far and wide to all the people of my little firm; Emma's acting group in London; Rowena Flakfizer, Penelope Tee, and a few of my friendly publisher clients; my editor, newly in possession of the latest Jefferson Honeywell manuscript, which she had phoned me up to tell me she thought was the best installment yet; Emma's mother's best friend, who ran the family bridal shop; my mother and her new husband in Australia; some law school friends I had kept in touch with; Dorothy Plum of the British embassy; Sophie Gleason; and an assortment of others who had touched our lives. As she had done for me, I also sent Violet Dixon an invitation, and though she declined to attend, she sent back a truly lovely and gracious note, with a subtle joke about her father that I was genuinely thrilled to see her feel free enough from his clutches to make—and myself to receive.

There was never a better place for a wedding than the rolling lawn that captured the entire expanse between the Eppses' lovely two-story Colonial house and the water's edge. Charlie made it clear that he alone was responsible for planning the wedding, which was set for a Saturday evening, with Doc Lou to conduct the ceremony. It was planned that Emma and I would go to our place in Connecticut on the Friday before the event.

I arranged that Ronnie and I would pick up Emmy in my Subaru on that Friday afternoon. The weeks of preparation had made her regret that she had agreed to ever give up the clerk's office. Me too. Five members of her troupe had arrived from London and we were putting them up overnight at the local inn. Lois's boyfriend, Tim, and Tim's trio of bass, drums, and keyboard would set up for the music. Rooms were also available at the inn for anyone who wanted to stay over and avoid late driving, but it was easy to come and go by rail, just an hour out of Grand Central.

Ronnie picked me up at my apartment and we headed for Gramercy Park to get Emma for the drive to Connecticut. He took a shortcut through Central Park, but when we stopped for a red light near the zoo, the car door was yanked open and a masked man gestured to me to get out. I did, taking my travel bag with me. On the side of the road were two motorbikes with sidecars. I was taken to one of the bikes and directed to get into the sidecar. The men mounted the bikes and took off. A short distance away was an automobile with a driver. I was helped out of the sidecar into the automobile and immediately driven to a reserved parking space, where the doors opened and passengers crowded into the front seat, middle seat, and backseat next to me. Snug against me was a mother with a curious child who inspected me, poking me this way and that, trying to fish in my pockets. The mother made no attempt to constrain him. The car made stops, passengers getting off and on with no apparent rhyme or reason.

It finally made a stop in the middle of a very crowded space, with bustling traffic, buses, food carts, cows, horse-drawn carts and vehicles, vendors, and sidewalks bulging with pedestrians patronizing the shops. The doors of my car opened and all the passengers spilled into the pedestrian mass. My driver put a sign on his windshield and left, taking his key from the dashboard. He closed all the doors, and I tried to talk to him but he took off. I had an uneasy feeling I had been here before. I got out of the car and reached in my pocket for some money to bribe my way to Gramercy Park, but my billfold was gone and my pockets were empty. My mind flipped to the mother and her inquisitive son rifling through my pockets. Well, nothing I could do about it now. With my travel bag in hand I navigated the pedestrian flow and found a police officer standing on a corner. I started to ask him for help but he paid no attention to me as a van filled with policemen pulled up and he got in and they took off. I stood there on the busy sidewalk with the pedestrians flowing around me, entreating them for help, but although a few looked at me, no one stopped. I was somewhat frightened but persisted, holding out my wristwatch as a lure as I called for help. Night had descended, and street- and shop lights were coming to life. I was hungry and thirsty and perplexed. I began to think about the wedding as a Subaru stopped in front of me with its door open. I got in.

"That you, Ronnie?"

"Yes, sir. You dozed off."

The car was pulling up to the entrance of Emma's apartment building.

"Ronnie, did men with masks stop the car, make me get out?"

"No, Mr. Tremaine. We had a very smooth ride."

Emma was waiting in the lobby with her bags, which Viktor carried out to the car. I reached in my pocket and to my relief found my wallet was there. I gave Viktor a generous tip.

Since she was taking a new substance called scopolamine prescribed by her doctor, Emma's Ménière's was doing much better with the ride to Connecticut. Also, her weekly experimental session in New York seemed to be helping.

"Dr. Litman had me to lunch," she told me as the car got on I-95. "What a charming, knowledgeable gentleman he is, certainly fond of you, which shows good taste. Said we needed to have lunch because he always likes to know the people he marries. He says he's bringing a lady with him to our wedding, a young chick of eighty-two who still sings at the Met. By the way, I brought something I once sang in a Gilbert and Sullivan show for you and me."

"Oh, I don't know . . ."

"You have a very nice voice," she said in a commanding tone, and she handed me a piece of paper with the words on it. "Is your mother coming?" she asked.

"No, sent her regrets, more of the same: it's just too far to go at her age. But she's sending a wedding present of a dozen frozen lamb chops from her husband's lamb chop company."

Emma said, "I'm so grateful that Molly"—this was her mother's former partner at Here Comes the Bride—"could make the trip. And *you* can't see it yet, but let me tell you, she's here bringing me the most divine wedding dress she's created for me. I don't think it's cheating," she added teasingly, "to tell you that it's light pink, with a short skirt, billowy at the shoulders, a ribbony thingee for my neck and hair . . ."

"And I'm wearing my favorite jacket with the sleeve back in place, a new burgundy bow tie and shirt, and a big white rose in the jacket's lapel."

"What a simply divine couple we will be!" She spun around and plunked her head on my lap, closed her lovely eyes, and promptly dozed off.

CHAPTER THIRTY

We pulled into the Eppses' driveway as the early shades of evening were starting to fall. The parking area across from the house was filled with the cars of guests for our wedding. A hum of voices and music greeted us. Emma went into the house, where she would remain until the ceremony began. I went to the wedding area, where I was to function as a kind of greeter, although Charlie was the designated host. The entire front of the house had been turned into a stunning panorama. Charlie had really outdone himself for us. The grounds were covered with multicolored lanterns, and hooded candles peppered the lawn like regimented dandelions. Dinner tables beflowered and illuminated with candles in hurricane lamps were arranged around a sleek surface laid over the grass for dancing. At the end of the lawn, its back to the surf, was a lovely altar for Doc Lou to preside over. Intertwined plants and flowers infused with multicolored stones highlighted the altar. All of it had the fragrance of the incumbent dinner wafting over it. A white-jacketed barman presided over a well-stocked dispensary, and hors d'oeuvres were making the rounds. I was surprised by the number of guests, quite beyond what I had anticipated. I thought the distance from New York would deter them, but I guess many lawyer friends and business associates wanted to see me finally submit to the yoke of matrimony. As the evening darkened, the torches and lanterns were illuminated above the lighted candles in the grass, and Lois's boyfriend, Tim, and his "Triple Threats" began to play seriously, which was the signal for everyone to freshen their drinks and occupy the chairs in front of the altar.

The band tapered off and Doc Lou took his place at the altar. "Good evening, all," he said. "I'm Dr. Louis Litman, a doctor of medicine who's also ordained to perform marriages, which have mostly been on behalf of my patients. In fact, this is my fiftieth such marriage, and it's for a young man who's been my patient since he was a boy, and his deceased father before him. It's my great joy to wed him tonight to a remarkable young woman from London. As a man of medicine I am fully aware of their mutual needs, but as a man of marriage I am equally aware of how, in trying circumstances, the infusion of an uplifting marriage can be a great facilitator. And that facilitation is love, not something that I can prescribe from the drugstore but something I can recognize and esteem this evening. They seek to bind their love into this marriage, and they have asked you to participate in their moment of joy, the start of their new life together. Swallows will fly, rosebuds burst open, apples turn red, joining our celebration. Please start the music."

I went to stand beside Doc Lou as Tim began to play on his keyboard. Emma, in her lovely pink dress, carrying a bouquet of gardenias, with Lydia beside her, came from the house down the row of candles and torches to the altar, a beguiling sight. Everyone applauded as she stood before Doc Lou and he put his arms around the two of us. "After fifty years of guiding couples into matrimony, none has resounded with me like yours. So it is fitting that I have decided that this will be my final marriage. I have learned much from doctoring people—about everything from suffering to the recoupment of good health—and I have had a great joy in uniting happy couples in matrimony. Now, in my eighty-ninth year, I have this wonderful farewell marriage to perform for a man who is as close to me as my own son, and for a splendid woman with whom he is going to spend the rest of his life. Chet Tremaine, please place the ring on your bride's finger."

Charlie, who was standing beside me, handed me the antique ring that Emma and I had chosen. I had a little trouble sliding it on her finger. Emma, when similarly commanded and handed a ring by Lydia, slipped hers on my finger with ease.

Doc Lou said, "Are you, Emma Vicky, and you, Chet Tremaine, ready to exchange your vows?"

We both said we were.

"Please proceed."

Emma smiled at me and we closely faced each other. I was as nervous as a cat caught in a bramble bush.

Emma: "None shall part us from each other—"

Me: "One in life and death are we."

Emma: "All in all to one another—"

Me: "I to thee and thou to me!"

Emma: "Thou the tree and I the flower—"

Me: "Thou the idol; I the throng—"

Emma: "Thou the day and I the hour—"

Me: "Thou the singer; I the song!"

Together: "None shall part us from each other, one in life

and death are we: All in all to one another—I to thee and thou to me!"

Beaming, Doc Lou said: "With the authority vested in me, I now pronounce you husband and wife."

Emma came into my arms, and when our lips pressed together the faint taste of teardrops came through the kiss. The band erupted with happy music and a rousing cry rose from the guests, who crowded us both with hugs and kisses, igniting the celebration that would take us into the night. I had never felt such jubilation, such unadulterated joy—they were happy for us, as happy as we were ourselves. I caught Emma's hand and started to dance with her, which enticed everyone to the dance floor with much cutting in and out.

The lights turned up as dinner was announced. No ordinary wedding dinner, not with Charlie Epps in charge. A full-blown clambake, suckling pigs straight from the twirling pits onto decorated platters, pheasants adorned with their plumage, hot biscuits, an endless flow of gustatory surprises. Emma and I were at a table with Lydia and Charlie himself near the dance floor, in full view of all of our guests. Emma said she felt like Cleopatra. Toasts began popping up from table to table to table. Also some self-induced entertainment. The three British actresses in their billowy dresses took to the dance floor and sang "I Could Have Danced All Night," with a marvelous whirling and dipping choreography to accompany it. Doc Lou was next with a very funny "Mad Dogs and Englishmen," giving it a quite good English accent. Then Doc's eighty-two-year-old Met youngster, Melinka Marova, took over with a full-blown rendition of an aria from *Carmen*, with Tim and company's accompaniment, her big operatic voice and rhythmic movement giving everyone a thrill. The two London actors followed in her wake with an amusing acrobatic tap dance, with lively improvised support from Tim's trio.

The lights fell low and a searchlight illuminated a huge sculptured wedding cake being wheeled in to the oohs and aahs of the assembled admirers. As the cake was being served, a small flat raft was anchoring offshore and a stunning barrage of fireworks began to paint the sky with a stream of fiery, floating, dripping, interactive beauties. There was a checkerboard of fountains, fighting bears exploding, an airplane doing loop-de-loops—all magic in the sky, with a farewell shower of arrows shooting every which way, lighting up the night.

A cry of approval shimmied up from us spectators. Charlie turned up the lights and announced: "How about a midnight swim?" The swimming pool lights above and below the water came on. There were plenty of takers heading toward the pool, while others went to the bar for refills. Doc Lou, a foaming beer in hand, was still doing remembrances of Noël Coward. Meanwhile, Sophie Gleason, my Nepal sponsor, was at the keyboard singing a torrid "Too Damn Hot" to her own bang-bang accompaniment.

"Well, Mrs. Wife," I said to Emma, "what do you say?"

"I say, Mr. Husband, we tiptoe away throwing farewell kisses to the wind for everyone." Emma took my ring hand, put it on top of hers, and said, "This is a dream, isn't it?"

"Of course."

"What happens when we wake up?"

"We won't."

"How come?"

"We're dream makers."

"We are, aren't we?"

"You betcha! One small dream after another."

Ronnie had brought the car into the driveway. No one saw our departure. Emma was a bit Ménière wobbly as I helped her into the backseat and the Subaru pulled away. Bhairav and goddess Kishani sat on top of the dashboard, facing us. I asked Ronnie to stop on Surf Road, which runs along the water. I stood up on the seat and opened the full hatch in the roof. I lifted Emma up and we stood side by side, arms around each other, our faces to the sky.

"Let's take a slow drive the long way along the water, Ronnie," I said, and cued up the copy of the goddess Kishani's recording that I had put on my phone.

Her soft voice began to serenade the night. A panoply of stars hung low overhead and a gentle surf wind played on our faces.

"I just saw a shooting star," Emma said. "Look, there goes another! Oh, what a heavenly wedding, wasn't it?"

"Yes, with one exception," I said.

"What can that possibly be?"

"Lifting you up, just now, I ripped off that same damn sleeve."

I raised the sleeve above our heads, letting it fly in the wind, our wedding banner.

ACKNOWLEDGMENTS

The Hotchner family would like to thank Nan Talese for standing beside Hotch from the beginning of his career till the very end. Paul Bresnick also never stopped believing in Hotch from the moment he started representing him. Thank you, Paul. Anna Kaufman, our editor, put her soul and her talents into this book, and the family will be forever grateful for her efforts reflected in these pages. We also salute Dan Novack for his words, sharp wit, and legal expertise. The family would also like to thank the good folks at Anchor: publisher Suzanne Herz; our publicity and marketing team, Julie Ertl and Annie Locke; the fabulous production team, including Barbara Richard, Edward Allen, Carolyn Williams, Aja Pollock, Rima Weinberg, NaNá Stoelzle, and Nicholas Alguire; and the magical, indefatigable cover designer, Michael Windsor. Finally, this book could not have been completed without Mara Neville-Abercrombie's constancy and intellect, Ana and Rony Trabanino's daily care and big hearts, and Monica Naryko's strength, spirit, and patience.